SCAREPLANE

book seven of the matchmaker mysteries series

elise sax

Scareplane (Matchmaker Mysteries – Book 7) is a work of fiction. Names, characters, places, and incidents are the products of the author's imagination or are used fictitiously. Any resemblance to actual events, locales, or persons, living or dead, is entirely coincidental.

Cover design: Elizabeth Mackey
Edited by: Novel Needs and Lynn Mullan
Formatted by: Jesse Kimmel-Freeman

Printed in the United States of America

elisesax.com
elisesax@gmail.com
http://elisesax.com/mailing-list.php
https://www.facebook.com/ei.sax.9
@theelisesax

For love and everything that comes with it.

ALSO BY ELISE SAX

PROLOGUE

The doorbell rang while I was changing out of my maid of honor dress into yoga pants and one of Spencer's sweaters. I had given Spencer a couple of drawers and half of my closet space since he had more or less moved in with me, but I regularly stole his socks, sweaters, sweats, and t-shirts. It was good to peel off the pretty dress and slip into comfortable clothes. As police chief, Spencer was busy with the aftermath of my friend Lucy's wedding and the flood that had washed away table settings for two hundred, the band's bassoon and oboe, twenty pairs of shoes, and a mountain of Jordan almonds. The last I heard, he and his police force were directing traffic around the debris on the highway outside of town, and miraculously, no one had been hurt in the natural disaster.

Meanwhile, Lucy was on her way with her new husband to a cruise ship docked in Long Beach, and I was stripping down and ready to binge watch Golden Girls reruns on television.

The doorbell rang again.

My grandmother stuck her head in my bedroom as I slipped on a pair of Spencer's socks. "Can you get that, dolly?" she asked. "It's Jean the real estate lady, and she wants to talk to you." Even though Grandma couldn't see who was at the door, she had a way of knowing things that couldn't be known.

"What does she want? I can't buy property." My credit score was slightly less than Bernie Madoff. I had to beg my bank to give me a debit card, and I still wasn't allowed to write checks since an unfortunate event a few years back.

"She wants to talk about somebody buying property for you."

"What?"

The doorbell rang again, and this time, it was followed by a loud knock on the door. "You better go, bubbeleh," Grandma said. "Jean's the most persistent woman I've ever known. She could get the dead to rise again if she needed them to sign mortgage papers."

"I have to sign mortgage papers?" I asked, slightly panicked, but my grandmother didn't answer. Instead she pointed her finger down the hallway toward the stairs.

I flew down the stairs as the doorbell rang yet again. I opened the front door, and sure enough, Jean the real estate lady was there. She was beautifully dressed in a power suit, and she had a large designer bag slung over her shoulder, which was filled with file folders.

"There you are," she said, clearly annoyed. "I thought you were dead or something, like maybe you were washed away."

"I got to higher ground in time," I explained.

"Good. Come with me."

She turned around and marched down the driveway. Jean was all business. I heard that real estate literally ran through her veins. She wasn't good at accepting no for an answer. I closed the door behind me and jogged after her. "What's happening? Where are we going?" I asked as I followed her.

"Over there, of course," she said, pointing at the house across the street.

The house across the street had been the scene of two murders, and after a complete renovation months ago, had been left abandoned and allowed to fall into disrepair. The front door was open and swinging in the wind. The front yard was overrun with weeds, and there was a swampy smell around it, probably from the pool in back.

Jean marched across the street and stopped on the sidewalk in front of the unfortunate house.

I put my hands on my hips. I had walked over in Spencer's socks, and they had taken a beating from the street. Spencer was going to kill me when he saw them. I was debating whether I should throw them away before he saw them or hide them in the back of his drawer and deny any knowledge of what caused their demise.

"What's going on? Is there a problem with the house? I don't even know who owns it now."

"It's stuck in probate," Jean explained. "But it's about to be unstuck. That's just the tip of this iceberg, Gladie."

"There's an iceberg?"

Jean grabbed my left hand and inspected my fingers. "He hasn't asked you, yet. That's what I figured."

"He? Who? What?"

"The cop. The chief."

"The…" Oh. Wait a second. The world spun around, but I willed myself not to faint. I clutched Jean's arms, pulled her close, and got in her face. "What have you heard? Spit it out."

Jean pulled away from me and smoothed out her power suit. A small smile appeared on her face, a sign of her delight at having personal information about me that I was desperate to know.

"Okay," she started. "Your honey has been looking at the house."

"Looking? What do you mean? Like he's been gazing at it while he runs in the mornings?"

"Like he's been asking around about the probate schedule and possible pricing."

"But he owns a condo," I said.

Her smile grew like a Cheshire cat's. "I know. I sold it to him."

"The house is so big, five times the size of his condo."

"I know," she said. "Why do you think he would need the extra space?"

Not for his baseball card collection, I was assuming.

"Listen," Jean continued. "This is the biggest house on the street. And it has a pool. So, I need to know if you're on board, because if you are, I'm going to push this thing all the way. If you're not, I've got other fish to fry. Do you get me?"

"No." I was hearing the rush of air in my ears, and my heart was pounding in my chest. "What're you saying? Fish? I'm so confused."

Jean turned me to face the house. "This is a family house, Gladie. This is what men buy for their wives. For their families. A big house with a pool and room for a kiddies' swing-set."

"A kiddies' swing-set. For their wives."

"So, what do you think?"

The house was beautiful. Large and every woman's dream.

But how could I own a house? I had never owned anything, except for my car, and I technically didn't pay a penny for that. Houses were permanent. Kind of like husbands.

Husbands.

Kiddies' swing-sets.

Spencer.

I love him, but…

"The house is bad luck," I told Jean.

She blinked, like I had gone out of focus. "What do you mean?"

"Two people were murdered there."

"So? What's your point?" she demanded. "That's nothing compared to the history of your grandmother's house. That one's like the Amityville Horror, but scarier."

"I don't think Grandma would live in the Amityville Horror," I said but wondered if there was some truth to what Jean said. "But this house is definitely bad luck… What's that sound?"

Jean scowled like a woman who was watching her six-percent take leave for good. "The only thing I hear is my retirement getting further away. Listen, I know houses. This one has good bones. The second you move in, it'll go up in value by at least thirty percent. You know what kind of investment that is, Gladie?"

I rubbed my ears and wondered if I was getting a cold. They were buzzing something awful. "I don't know about investments. I worked on Wall Street, but that was only dressed up as a hot dog and handing out fliers for a diner for four days."

Jean stomped her foot and pointed at the house, again. "Well, take it from me. I have two mill in an index fund, and I can tell you that this house is an investment of a lifetime. It's not bad luck. There's no such thing as a bad luck house. It's good luck. Not bad luck. Good luck. Do you hear me? Good luck. Good luck. Good luck. This house is good luck. What's that sound?"

"You hear it, too?" I asked.

"It sounds like killer bees on the loose. Killer bees would be bad luck, but I have a great bee guy who can handle them for a reasonable fee."

The sound got louder. I took a tentative look up, searching the skies above me for bees, but there were none. There was something worse.

"Oh my God," I said.

"Oh my God," Jean said.

A small plane was falling from the sky with a trail of black smoke behind it. It was making the loud bee sound, and it was getting louder, as it got closer to crashing on our heads.

"We should run," I suggested.

"It's not going to hit us," Jean said, ever the optimist. Despite her positive attitude, she put her hands over her head, shielding it.

I didn't think her hands would be enough to protect her from a plane landing on her head. The plane was heading right for us, but it could have veered off at any point, so even if we ran, there was no guarantee we would be safe.

"We're going to die," Jean breathed, her optimism flying out the window as the plane got closer.

"We're not going to die," I said, patting her back.

"I'm not an idiot Gladie," she spat at me. "I know that you die when a plane crashes on you."

"I mean, maybe it won't hit us. Maybe it's not crashing. Maybe it's doing some kind of acrobatic trick, like in an air show, or a movie from the 1920s about airplanes."

Jean seemed to think about that for a moment. "You think so?"

"Sure," I said, but I was a big fat liar. The plane was above us and coming down fast. It was definitely crashing, and we were in its path. "Hit the deck!" I shouted and tackled Jean to the ground.

I shut my eyes tight as I covered Jean with my body. I tried to remember a prayer, but all I could think of was the prayer for eating bread, which made me remember that my grandmother had leftover cinnamon buns in the refrigerator. Why hadn't I eaten the cinnamon buns? Now I was going to get crushed to death, craving cinnamon buns. Damn diets. If I lived, I was never going to diet ever again. Oh, who was I kidding? There was no way I was going to survive.

Then, it happened. The plane crashed. The noise was terrible. Just like a plane crashing into a house. A bad luck house.

As the thought hit me, I knew exactly what had happened. I pushed down on Jean's head as I struggled to stand. Sure enough, the plane had crashed right into the biggest house on the block. The back half of the house was gone, and now there was only a plane with its tail sticking straight up. But the front half of the house was completely intact. The plane was damaged, but there was no fire and not even a wisp of any more smoke.

"Where's the fire?" I asked. "Is it going to blow up?"

Jean grabbed hold of my hand and pulled herself up. Her hair was messed up, and she had a bruise on her face, which was probably my fault. "The house," she said. "It killed the house. The plane went after it like it had it in for it."

"The house is bad luck," I said and took a couple steps toward the front door.

Jean pulled me back. "Where are you going?"

"I'm going to see if they're okay," I said, pointing at the plane. There was the distant sound of sirens coming our way. Two police cars and an ambulance. I recognized the sounds after all of my experiences with emergency services.

"One of them is okay, but he has a broken leg," my grandmother called from behind me. She was standing in her driveway, watching me. I gave her the okay signal.

"I can't believe a plane crashed through the house while I was standing here," Jean said and gave me a pointed look. "You did this."

"Excuse me?" I asked, blinking.

"You didn't want the house, so you cursed it. You cursed the house."

"I don't curse houses, Jean. I told you it was bad luck."

"You cursed it," she said and crossed herself.

I rolled my eyes. "Jean, you're Jewish."

"You can't be too careful," she said. "You're not going to curse me, too, are you?"

The police cars arrived, with Spencer's unmarked car leading the way. He parked on the street by me and hopped out. "Are you okay?" he asked me and searched my body for damage.

"Jean thinks I'm a witch," I told him.

"Smart woman," Spencer said.

"Grandma said there's a survivor, but he has a broken leg," I said.

Spencer nodded and ordered the paramedics to save the man, but before they moved toward the house, the front door flew open all the way, and a man popped out.

He was about forty years old with brown hair, and he was wearing khaki shorts and a blue golf shirt. "I'm alive," he said, leaning against the door frame. "The plane crashed, but I'm alive. I'm alive, right?"

The paramedics rushed to him, and Spencer and the other police ran to the plane to check out the ones who weren't so lucky.

It turned out that the survivor was Arthur Fox, a caterer from Northern California, who was so thrilled at his luck to survive a plane crash that at that moment, he decided to move to our town. The pilot and the other passenger didn't make it, though. The coroner later said they died on impact.

The house across the street stayed in probate, and the plane stayed in the house while the authorities tried to figure out who was responsible for what.

"It's a clusterfuck," my grandmother explained to me later that evening, as we watched Golden Girls and ate the leftover cinnamon buns. "They won't figure it out for weeks. We might as well get used to a view of a plane in the middle of that bad luck house."

"Those poor people," I said. "You never know when it's your time."

My thoughts went to the vacation that Spencer and I were

going to take in a few weeks and the plane that we would take to get there. Grandma took my hand in hers on her lap. "Sometimes it's good not to know," she said.

CHAPTER 1

There's all kinds of matches and all kinds of reasons why matches come to us to be matched. Some are lonely. Some are suckers for love. But some just want something new. Something exciting. Just like eating a spicy meal or riding a thrilling roller coaster, people get a kick out of being scared. And new is scary, bubbeleh. New is different. When we're unhappy, we think that different has to be better. Mashed potatoes and fried chicken may not be spicy, but they're still delicious, comforting, and familiar. How can you get better than that? But it's not so bad to be scared a little here and there and try a chipotle burrito for a change, dolly. Sure, you'll get a nasty case of heartburn, but then you can eat your fried chicken again later, sure in the knowledge that it's just as good as spicy food and there's no diarrhea, either. Diarrhea's scary, but your matches will get it and there's nothing you can do about it. So, when they want new and scary, give it to them, but I'll bet dollars to donuts that they'll be back to mashed potatoes in no time.

Lesson 12, Matchmaking advice from your

Something was terribly wrong. Spencer wasn't feeling me up, trying to get in a quickie before breakfast like he did every morning.

With my eyes closed, I patted the bed next to me, but it was empty, just lonely sheets with the blanket crumpled in a heap at the foot of the bed. I opened my eyes and sat up. Spencer was putting the finishing touches on his tie in front of the mirror in the corner.

Spencer was a hot metrosexual who wore a suit better than any GQ cover model. With his tie fixed, he slipped his suit jacket on and buttoned it.

"What's happening?" I asked him. "Did someone die?"

"No, and nobody better die until next week. I don't want anything to go wrong during the law enforcement conference."

I rolled my eyes, adjusted my pillow, and scooted my body backward so that I could lean against the headboard. Spencer was the chief of police of our small town of Cannes, California, which was high up in the mountains, east of San Diego. Spencer wasn't thrilled with his police force on a good day, and now he was hosting a law enforcement conference, and he had been freaking out about it for the past week, sure that the town or his employees would embarrass him.

He put his wallet and phone in his jacket's inside pocket and his gun and shield on his waistband. Then, he stopped and arched an eyebrow while he gave me the once over. He smirked his usual smirk.

"I'm rethinking the quickie thing," he said. "You look damned good in my bed, Pinky."

"Your bed? I thought this was my bed."

"Squatter's rights. Look it up." His phone dinged, and he read the message on its screen. "Oh, damn. Gotta go," he said, serious again.

"You've been working nonstop. Is Remington still out of town?"

"Yes, but that's okay. I've got someone taking up the slack," he said and gave me a quick kiss. "I might not make it home for dinner. Busy. Busy."

"That's okay. I'm busy, too. I have two new matches to meet at Tea Time," I said to Spencer's back, as he walked out of the room.

"Everyone loves the matchmaker who can curse a house," he said and disappeared down the hall. I sighed. Spencer was joking, but he was right. A good chunk of the town now believed that I could curse a building ever since the house across the street had been hit by an airplane a few weeks before. Funny thing was, cursing was good for the matchmaking business. I guessed they figured that if I could make a plane fly into a house, I could find them their true love.

After hopping in the shower, I went downstairs. My grandmother was waiting for me in the kitchen. "Good morning, dolly," she greeted me in her blue housedress. "I got the bagels in the toaster. Would you put on the coffee?"

"Sure. Spencer had to leave early to prepare for his conference."

"I know. He said goodbye before he left," Grandma said, taking the bagels out of the toaster and putting them on plates on the table. She took a seat and began to spread cream cheese on her bagel. I poured coffee into our mugs and took the milk out of the refrigerator. "Another busy day for matchmaking?"

"It's been nonstop for weeks, ever since you know what."

We turned our heads in unison in the direction of the house next door. The plane crash was still caught in the mess of law enforcement, the FAA, the TSB, and probate, and so the plane wreckage was still sitting in the middle of the house with its tail sticking up in the air like a flagpole, announcing to the town about my powers to curse large structures.

"You're making love matches, dolly. That's a good thing, no matter why the matches come to you."

I hoped she was right. In addition to making love matches, I was finally making real money. For the first time in forever, my bank account was in the black. I was even considering buying new clothes for the change of seasons.

I washed the dishes and kissed Grandma goodbye. I had an appointment with a new match in ten minutes, which was just enough time to walk to Tea Time, the tea shop where I had been doing most of my business lately.

I left the house and took a deep breath of the sweet mountain spring air. It was March in Cannes, and the weather was sensual in its perfectness. Cannes was a small town, which had been founded in the 19th century after gold was discovered. But the gold ran out quickly, and today Cannes was a haven for tourists looking for antique stores and pie shops and a walk around the apple and pear orchards. My grandmother's house was one of the oldest houses in the tourist-invaded Historic District, and it was a beautiful Victorian, but tourists weren't taking pictures of it today. Instead, they were hovering on the sidewalk across the street, taking selfies in front of the house with the plane sticking up out of it. There were at least a dozen tourists, which was pretty typical for any given time since the crash. The house had gotten a lot of attention, and it had even been the lead story on CBS Sunday Morning.

I walked quickly past the tourists, hoping they didn't point at me and mutter *curse curse*, which had been happening lately. I walked so fast that I got to Tea Time five minutes early.

The tea shop was located in the Historic District and housed in an old saloon. It still had the original bar from its Wild West days and a few bullet holes in a wall. Tea Time sold expensive tea and Cannes's best coffee, much to the frustration of its owner, Ruth Fletcher, who thought that coffee drinkers were one notch above serial killers. I had a deal with Ruth for free lattes for a year, and I was taking advantage of it in spades.

Opening the door to Tea Time, I raised my hand. "Large latte for here, Ruth!" I called.

Ruth was an ornery octogenarian with more energy than I had. Her hair was cut short, and she had no makeup on her face. She was wearing Katharine Hepburn pants, a men's short-sleeved button-down shirt, and pearls.

"Shut up!" she hollered at me. "You think you own the place or something?"

"Just the lattes," I said happily, taking a seat at a center table. The place was packed, and it was the only free table. Despite her complaints, Ruth started up the espresso machine. Her grand-niece Julie was waiting the tables.

"Tea is hot," she squeaked as she passed me. I noticed her hands were bandaged, and the teapot she carried was sloshing tea out as she walked.

Ruth plopped down across from me and handed me my latte. I took a sip. "Delicious," I told her. Ruth sneered back at me.

"Coffee will kill you, Gladie."

"Yes, but what a way to go."

Ruth looked at Julie and shook her head. "I wonder how long it will take that girl to figure out to put the lids on the teapots. At least she hasn't set fire to anything for a few days. Look at this place. Packed with tourists. My dogs are barking, and it's barely eight o'clock."

She was right. We were having a more than usual busy start to the tourist season. "I heard there were tour buses coming up from L.A. to see the wildflowers."

Ruth nodded and wiped a hand down her face. "They say we've got the biggest wildflower bloom in eighty years. God save us from the Daffodil Committee. Those freaks are the worst. I wish I could hibernate until May."

"Daffodil Committee?" I asked, but there was a crash in the back room, and Ruth went to see what damage her niece had done.

"Gladie? Gladie Burger?"

A middle-aged man with dark curly hair, who was wearing a blue suit with half of a tie and a hopeful expression, was standing over me.

"I'm Gladie," I said. "Are you Mr. Doughy?"

He nodded and offered me his hand to shake. "Call me Larry. Phew. I'm so glad I found you."

He took a seat at my table and blew out air. His breath smelled like toothpaste, and I figured he was meeting with me on his way to work. I took a sip of my latte and pushed down the nervous feeling I still got when faced with a client. People were coming to me to help them with big life decisions and to help them be happy, and I wasn't sure I was all that competent.

"How can I help you, Larry?" I asked in my most professional voice.

He smoothed out his half-tie and looked down at it, self-consciously. "A cat ate it," he explained to me. "On my way here."

"A cat ate your tie on your way to see me?" I took another sip of my latte.

"Yep. It jumped into my car and ate my tie. That's kind of why I called you to match me."

Because I was good with cats? Because I had a tie collection? Neither of those was true. Larry Doughy was going to be so disappointed.

He leaned forward and grabbed my wrist. "I'm cursed," he whispered. His eyes were round saucers, and his pupils were dilated.

"You're cursed," I repeated calmly, smiling, and nodding my head like I dealt with cursed people all of the time. My phony courage aside, I scanned the shop for Ruth because she had a Louisville Slugger ready if the situation warranted it, and even if it didn't warrant it.

"I've been cursed for the past nine days, ever since I wrote that tweet. It's been a doozy of nine days, I got to tell you. I got to get this curse lifted 'cause I only have so many toes."

Larry kicked his right foot up onto the table and took his shoe and sock off. I counted his toes.

Three.

"I won't even tell you what happened to the other two," he said, pointing to his unfortunate foot. There were a series of stitches where the other two toes used to be.

I looked around nervously for Ruth. "You'd better put your foot away," I urged. "Ruth is particular about not having feet on her tables."

He put his sock and shoe back on. "You're my only chance."

"I'm sure I can find a match for you who doesn't care about your toes," I assured him.

Larry leaned forward. His expression was that of a desperate man. "Match me? I want you to uncurse me."

"I...huh?"

"Uncurse me. I heard about the house. Just do the opposite of what you did to the house."

It took fifteen minutes to convince Larry Doughy that I could match him and bring love into his life, which would take the edge off his whole curse thing. But as far as Larry Doughy was concerned, I was the witch who could free him of whatever curse was on his head from unwise tweeting. So, I agreed to a swap in which I would do my best to uncurse him if he let me match him, too. It wasn't an ideal arrangement, but he gave me a check for two hundred dollars as a down payment, so who was I to argue about my uncursing talents?

As soon as Larry left Tea Time, Ruth attacked my table with a spray bottle of disinfectant and a wad of paper towels. "I've had a lot of things on my tables, Gladie," she grumbled. "But this was the first time I've had a three-toed foot on it."

"You sprayed my latte, Ruth. I'll need another one."

"Aren't you leaving? It's like your ass is glued to my antique chair."

"I have another match any second. A little more sugar in my latte this time, Ruth. Do you have any Danish?"

Ruth threw the paper towels at me. "This is a place of business. A business." She was spitting mad, and her wrinkly face was bright red.

"That's what I'm doing, Ruth. Business."

"*Your* business. But this is *my* business."

I rolled my eyes. "Tomay-to, tomah-to."

My next match walked in the door. Cynthia Andre was a retired county clerk from L.A., and she had recently moved to a cottage just outside of the Historic District of Cannes to find love and to needlepoint the great monuments of Europe.

I handed my latte cup to Ruth. "Make sure you clean it out," I told her. "I don't want to drink bleach, and don't forget the Danish. You got prune? I could use some prune."

Ruth rolled her eyes. "How long is this going to last, making my tea shop your office?"

"I hope forever. I'm an empire, Ruth. I'm the queen of matchmakers. I went to the gas station yesterday and filled up my tank all the way. All the way, Ruth. I'm a goddamned titan of industry."

She grabbed the latte cup from me. "I'll tell you this. Half this town thinks you have powers to crash a plane into an innocent house, but eventually it'll be the new season of *The Bachelor*, and they'll forget about your magical powers, and it'll be 'give me five dollars' worth of gas on number three' all over again. Meanwhile, Larry Doughy's digits aren't long for this world, and you're going to need to get him help before sandals season. Damned Twitter. I wouldn't get near that social media stuff if you paid me a million dollars."

"You really think he's cursed?" I asked her, surprised. Ruth was an Age of Reason fan and had probably even lived through the era. She often made fun of my grandmother's third eye. It wasn't like her to put stock in magic or curses.

"I think he's had a terrible run of bad luck, and it doesn't look like it's anywhere close to ending. Don't you know anything?"

she asked, but didn't wait around for an answer, not that I could have answered her.

I took Larry's check out of my purse and looked at it. Two hundred dollars. That was more than enough money to deal with a curse or a run of bad luck.

Cynthia looked around the shop for me, and I stood up and waved at her. "Over here," I called. She smiled at me and marched to the table like she was leading a battalion in the Russian Revolution. She plopped down on the chair across from me and slammed her utilitarian purse on the table.

"I want a man who can cook," she said. "Are you taking notes?"

I rifled through my purse for a scrap of paper and a pen. I jotted down a note about Cynthia's need for a cooking man.

"And he needs a full head of hair," she added and pointed at my paper for me to continue writing. "I don't want bald or half bald or comb-over. I want a thick head of manly hair, cut above the ear."

I ran out of room on the scrap of paper.

"I don't think that'll be a problem," I said, but I didn't know a single man her age who could cook and had hair anywhere besides his ears. I would have to get my grandmother's help for Cynthia. She knew everyone.

"I heard you were good," Cynthia said and then her voice

dropped to a whisper. "I heard you could do things."

"Well…" I started.

"And I heard that you're dating the chief of police. He's got nice hair."

She was right. Spencer had a gorgeous head of hair. Dark and thick and always perfectly cut. I blushed, thinking about his beautiful hair.

"That police station is like a modeling agency," Cynthia continued. "There's another one over there who looks like The Rock."

I blushed, again. She was talking about Remington Cumberbatch, who I had seen naked on more than one occasion before I started dating Spencer.

"And then the new one should be on a runway somewhere," Cynthia said.

"New one?"

"The new detective."

"Oh. Yes." I didn't know there was a new detective. Spencer had mentioned that he had help, but he didn't say it was a detective. In fact, he had been closed-lipped about work lately, except for the fact that he was freaking out about the conference. I was sort of surprised that he had hired another hottie for his force, especially after what had gone on between Remington and me.

"He's very good-looking, huh?"

"She. Detective Williams. She looks like Angelina Jolie but with bigger boobs and longer legs."

Ruth brought me my latte. "What's the matter, girl? Did you forget to breathe?" she asked me. "You got no color in your face."

I gasped and sucked in some air. "Bigger boobs than Angelina Jolie?" I asked Cynthia, ignoring Ruth.

"Are you talking about the new cop?" Ruth asked. "I hear they had to special order her uniforms. Probably at Sexy-Mama-R-Us or something. Men are going to start turning themselves in just to get frisked by her. Poor Fred had to go home early the other day because he was hyperventilating so bad after he caught a good look at the new cop walking away from him. I mean, she's got a butt that can stop traffic. You get me? Gladie? Gladie? Did you have a stroke?"

CHAPTER 2

Funny thing about jealousy, bubbeleh. Sometimes a person will be jealous when they shouldn't be and not be jealous when they should be. It's hard to tell a jealous person what to do. On one hand, don't worry about what you can't help and what probably is nothing because being jealous is a lot of energy. On the other hand, where there's smoke, there's fire. And getting burned hurts worse than a zetz on your tuchus.

Lesson 100, Matchmaking advice from your
Grandma Zelda

"It's probably nothing to worry about," I told Bridget in her condo. She was sitting at her dining room table with a client, doing his taxes. The table was covered in papers, her computer, and a large calculator. Bridget's condo was three stories, each a small floor. This was the eating floor. I opened her cabinets and searched for snack foods that would take my mind off of Detective Angelina Jolie's legs.

"Where are the goldfish crackers and Nutella? Isn't that what kids eat?"

"I don't have a kid yet. I have three months to go," Bridget said, pushing buttons on her calculator. "And little Lech isn't going to eat processed food. He's going to be vegan or paleo. I haven't decided yet."

"I don't want to pay taxes this year, Bridget," Bridget's client said. I recognized him as the owner of the cat ceramics store outside of the Historic District. "My daughter has a cross-bite. Do you realize how much that costs?"

Bridget pushed her hoot owl glasses up on the bridge of her nose. "I think you're going to have to pay taxes, Jerry, unless you have a lot of new deductions."

"Wait a minute," I said, still holding the pantry door open. "Who's Lick? You're naming your son Lick? I mean, not that there's anything wrong with that."

Phew. I had to catch myself. It wasn't safe to criticize parents. Bridget was my best friend, and I didn't want to ruin our relationship because I was freaked out by her weird baby names or the fact that she was never going to buy goldfish crackers, again. My stomach growled, and I went to the fridge to see what vegan / paleo people ate for snacks.

"Not Lick," Bridget explained, stretching out her back.

Her belly was getting bigger every day. "Lech. Like Lech Walesa, the Polish labor organizer. He was president, too, but I don't care about that."

"Lech," I said. "Nice name." Actually, it was better than her last name for her unborn baby, Vladimir.

"Aren't teeth a deductible?" Bridget's client asked her. "Teeth should be a deductible. Do you know how much teeth cost? They cost an arm and a leg!" he shouted without irony.

Bridget wiped her brow and tucked her curls behind her ear. She had a lot of hair, and it was growing like weeds since she got pregnant. "I don't think teeth are a deductible. Did you give to charity?"

"Charity?" he asked, his voice rising again. "How can I give to charity? Do you know how much teeth cost?"

I glided my tongue over my teeth, searching for expensive cavities or a cross-bite, whatever that was. Then, I spotted a jar of olives in the fridge and grabbed it. I brought it to the table and opened it.

"So, I don't have to worry, right?" I asked Bridget. "Just because Spencer hid the fact that he hired a hot female detective who has custom-made uniforms?"

Bridget's client whistled. "You talking about Detective Terri Williams? Now *she's* got nice teeth."

"How nice?" I asked, fear prickling my skin.

"Not as nice as her ass," he said, thoughtfully. He blushed. "Sorry. I forgot I was in mixed company."

"But I don't have to worry, right?" I asked.

"Spencer loves you," Bridget said. "He doesn't care about teeth or asses."

"Huh?" I said.

"I don't want to pay taxes," the client repeated, tapping the papers on the table.

Bridget exhaled. She looked exhausted. It was only March, and she had another month of tax season. She did pretty much everyone's books in town, and nobody liked taxes.

"Did you go to any cat ceramic conferences? Has your mileage increased to buy cat ceramics?"

I looked at the client, as he focused up at the ceiling, trying to create cat ceramic conferences out of thin air, I was assuming, in order not to pay taxes.

"I don't want to be a buttinski," I said. "But maybe this is a good break time. You can have time to think about deductions, and I can take Bridget to lunch."

"Oh, lunch sounds good," Bridget said. "I hear there's a new fair trade chef salad at Saladz."

"Yum. I love fair trade," I said.

The client thought about it a minute and finally nodded. "Okay, Bridget. I'll give it some thought and email you with my new expenses list."

Bridget looked relieved and rubbed her belly. "That sounds perfect," she said.

Bridget drove us in her Volkswagen Beetle. "Do you mind if we do a slight detour on our way to Saladz?" I asked her. Saladz was our normal lunch place with our friend, Lucy. The restaurant was located in the center of the Historic District, and it had good food and ample portions.

"No problem. Where to?"

"The police station."

Bridget turned left. "Oh, good. I've been meaning to talk to Spencer about the injustice of minimum sentencing."

"Good idea," I said, but I was thinking about Detective Terri Williams. Spencer had kept her a secret from me. Why? Did he think I would be jealous, just because she was stunningly gorgeous with perfect teeth? Or was he hiding something? Something between him and his beautiful new recruit?

"Park here!" I barked at Bridget.

"But it's police parking only."

"I sleep with the police chief. That's close enough. Park here!"

Bridget flinched, and her glasses fell off her face. The car swerved, and she tried to get it under control, steering wildly. The car finally came to a stop with the two right wheels up on the curb.

"Holy crap," Bridget said, putting the car into park.

"Is Lech okay?"

She rubbed her belly and searched for her glasses. "Yep. He's wedged in there pretty well."

"I'm sorry I scared you. I might be stressed."

"Well, you've been busy lately."

"That's true," I said. I had been working a lot lately. It had been nonstop matchmaking for weeks. But that wasn't why I was stressed. "To tell you the truth, Bridget, I might be stressed about Spencer."

"About the new detective?"

There was a knock on my window, but I ignored it and kept my focus on Bridget. I put my finger up behind me to tell whoever it was to wait. I was finally ready to confront my fears about Spencer. My real fears.

"I never told you about what Jean told me before the plane flew into the house," I started.

"Gladie, there's someone who wants to talk to us," Bridget said, as someone knocked on my window, again.

"They can wait," I said. "This is important. So, here's the thing…"

I was going to tell my best friend that Spencer had been shopping around for a family home. A home for a husband and wife. And logic dictated that Spencer would be the husband and I would be the wife. And then there was the whole thing about how I felt about it.

The knocking grew louder. "Gladie," Bridget said. "I think that I have to open the window."

I turned to look at who was interrupting me. As the window opened, I got a gander at the world's most beautiful woman. There was a breeze, and it whipped her hair in a perfect way, just like in a porno movie or a commercial for hair conditioner. It reminded me that when my frizzy hair got blown by the wind, I looked like a psychotic, electroshock patient. With the window open, I could smell the woman, too. Roses and chocolate cake. She was wearing a black power suit, and she had one hand wrapped around the arm of a young man with his hands handcuffed behind his back. Even though he was obviously being arrested, he looked like a pig in shit being so close to the most beautiful woman in the world.

"I think it's Angelina Jolie," Bridget whispered.

It wasn't Angelina Jolie. I knew exactly who it was. It was Detective Terri Williams, Ms. Perfect, the Other Woman.

"Get this car off the curb," she commanded. She had the whole tough cop thing going for her in spades, like Sipowitz in *NYPD Blue*. I didn't think it would take much for her to shoot us off the curb.

"We're just visiting," Bridget told her.

Detective Perfect blinked. "I don't care what you're doing. Move the car, or I'm going to arrest your ass."

"She's dating Spencer," Bridget continued, smiling. I elbowed her hard in her boob.

"We'll move," I croaked. All of the moisture in my mouth had evaporated in a cloud of humiliation and anger at Spencer. "Go, go, go," I hissed, and Bridget put the car into drive. The car hopped off the curb, and Bridget drove at a snail's pace in search for a legal parking spot.

"Now what?" she asked me after she turned the car off.

"We're going to find Spencer."

"Did you see that woman? Now I feel guilty for picketing magazine offices in New York for misrepresenting the female body on their covers. That woman looked exactly like she had been photoshopped. Maybe I've been wrong about what's possible all this time."

I patted her arm. "You weren't wrong," I said. "Obviously that woman is an alien from another planet or something. Or she's had major plastic surgery."

"If she did, her surgeon deserves the Nobel Prize or something."

"Damn it. You're right," I said, and searched my purse for lipstick, but I only found an old tube of chocolate-flavored lip balm. I needed industrial putty on my face to compete with Detective Perfect, but I only had chocolate-flavored lip balm. I didn't think it was enough to put me over the top. "You got any mascara?"

"Mascara is the Pol Pot of feminism."

I took that as a no.

That's how I walked into the police station with stubby eyelashes and chocolate-flavored lips. I didn't care if I was half the woman as Spencer's new detective. I mean, I cared a whole hell of a lot, but I had to see her with Spencer. I had to see if there was chemistry between them. I had to know if there was something to worry about.

And I had to shake my finger at Spencer and call him the dog that he was.

"Check my nose for boogers," I told Bridget, as we walked to the police station's front door. I was having second thoughts during the short trip from the parked car to the front door. Jealous women weren't given a lot of points when they stormed into their boyfriends' workplaces. I was panicking.

"All clear," she said, giving my nose a good look.

Best friends are the best.

I opened the police station door for Bridget and followed her inside. The station was housed in a new building, far nicer than one would expect for our tiny police force in our small town. The lobby was clean and shiny with two comfy chairs, facing the front desk. Bridget took a seat and balanced her purse on her belly. I waved to police officers that I knew as they ran back and forth with dusters in their hands. It looked like it was all hands on deck to prepare for the conference. Spencer had been worried that his police force would embarrass him, and he wanted to put his best foot forward as the host to five top cops from all over California.

Detective Hotness was barking orders at the desk sergeant while she kept her hand clutched around her prisoner's upper arm. The desk sergeant was Fred Lytton, my first match. His eyes flicked from left to right as he tried to take in all of Terri Williams's commands. I waved to him, and he waved back.

"Hello there, Underwear Girl," he called, smiling, perhaps relieved to see a friendly face.

Detective Flawless Skin turned around and scowled at me, looking me up and down in derision. I was tempted to explain the Underwear Girl nickname to her, but the explanation wasn't any better than what she was probably thinking.

"Is Spencer around?" I asked Fred.

"Sure thing. You want me to get him for you?"

"No, you won't, sergeant," Terri Williams roared. "You're

going to process this prisoner and you're going to do it now."

Fred gave me an "I'm sorry" look and shrugged his shoulders. I shrugged my shoulders right back at him. He walked around the desk and took the prisoner from the most beautiful mean person I had ever seen and walked toward the processing room.

"This is a place of business," she spat, approaching me with her arms crossed.

Why were people telling me that? I knew about business. I was a businesswoman. I made matches and was a standup citizen. "I'd like to see Spencer," I said, willing myself to maintain eye contact and not look away cowardly.

"The chief is busy working. If you have an emergency, I can help you."

I saw red. My blood boiled in my veins. My hands formed into fists. I had only gotten into a few fights in my life, but I was ready to take on Detective Gun-Toting Bitch in front of me. She was literally standing between me and seeing my boyfriend, the man who had shared my bed for nearly two months.

I stuck my finger up in the air. "I…" I started, but Fred interrupted me. He stepped out of the processing room with his hands in latex gloves, pointing to the ceiling, like he was a surgeon.

"Detective, I found something in his…in his…butt." Fred wiped his forehead with the back of his forearm. He looked like he was about to cry. I didn't blame him. I wouldn't want to search for contraband in criminals' butts. It was one of the few jobs that I had never had.

"Well, process it, sergeant," she responded, completely unconcerned.

"But, ma'am there's more stuff up in there."

He shuddered. Fred was definitely looking for a way out, but Detective Foxy Bossy wasn't going to give it to him, and he knew it. He hung his head in defeat and returned to the processing room.

"Now listen here," I started, again. "I can see Spencer Bolton whenever I want to."

"I told you, he's busy."

I stomped my foot like I was eleven years old. "I know he's busy. I'm wearing his socks!"

"Oh my God!" Fred wailed from the processing room. "It's like Carlsbad Caverns. The Holland Tunnel of butts. Don't you have a backpack? A plastic grocery bag? Why did you put all of this stuff up there?"

"Why is there a racket out here?" Spencer demanded, making an appearance in the lobby.

"Chief, this is…" Detective Bitchface Hottie began, but I cut her off, claiming my territory.

"Fred is digging items out of a criminal's butt, and I'm

here to *talk* to you."

I shot him my most withering stare, and I pursed my chocolate-flavored lips for added effect. Spencer visibly swallowed and looked from me to his new detective and back to me.

There it was. Guilt.

Spencer felt guilty about hiring the best-looking woman in the world and not telling me about it, which was tantamount to lying and definitely hiding. Now he was working with her, and she was preventing me from seeing him.

We'll just see about that.

"Hello, Gladie," he said, using my real first name instead of Pinky, which was his nickname for me. "Is something wrong? I mean, do you need me?"

I arched an eyebrow.

Fred stumbled into the lobby again and leaned against a wall for support. His gloved hands were still in the surgeon pose. "Fifteen items," he said, shaking his head, as if he was trying to erase the memory from his brain. "Fifteen items. And it's not done. It's like he uses his hiney as a storage unit."

"Sergeant, get back in there until the job's done," Detective Pitbull Babe barked at him, making him flinch.

"Fred, it can't be long now," Spencer told him, more gently. "My record for digging stuff out of a perp is forty-two. I'm sure that you're almost done."

Fred took a deep breath, and fortified with Spencer's words, went back into the processing room.

"It's sort of comforting," Bridget said from her chair. "I mean, if you can fit all of that in a rectum, pushing a baby out of a vagina shouldn't be too difficult."

She had a point, but I doubted one had anything to do with the other. Instead, I figured the perp probably had an extraordinary rectum. Otherwise, people would be storing stuff in their butts all the time.

I bent down and gave Bridget a half hug with one arm. She was a single mother, about to squeeze a human out of her crotch. Of course, she was nervous and worrying about the mechanics of the whole thing.

"Your OB GYN has the best drugs. She told me so," I said.

"Are we done here?" Detective Touchy Feely asked, impatient.

Spencer looked at me, and I thought I detected a flinch. At the very least, he was sheepish. He knew that his new hire was a problem. And a bitch. I had been raring to go with the riot act, but a new strategy was knocking on my brain. I could either be the furious, jealous girlfriend, who was understandably upset that her boyfriend lied to her, or I could be the above-it-all girlfriend, who was gracious under all circumstances and befriended the most beautiful bitch detective and spied on her boyfriend with a smile and without his knowledge or suspicions.

That way, if I found any hanky panky was going on, I would cut off Spencer's penis with a hacksaw.

"Oh yes," I said with the smile I used when I was trying to get out of a traffic ticket. "Bridget and I were just driving by on our way to lunch, and I thought it would be nice to say hello. And I'm so happy to meet you, Detective Williams," I said, sounding slightly like the Queen of England, taking her hand in both of mine, like I was a cult leader, and she was a hopeful recruit. "I just know that Spencer—I mean, Chief Bolton—will be in great hands with your professionalism."

"Make it stop! Make it stop!" Fred wailed from the processing room. "This is horrible! I should have been a forest ranger, like my mother wanted. Nobody puts things up their butt in a forest."

"And you must give me the name of your perfume," I continued to Detective Nasty Knockout. "You smell like an angel." I smiled even wider at her, and I felt Spencer's eyes on me. I stole a glance and saw his confused expression. He never would have expected that I would be diplomatic and gracious…and speak like the Queen of England when faced with his lie. *Figure that out, jerkface*, I thought. *Be afraid. Be very afraid.*

I dropped Detective Leggy Louse's hands and gave Spencer a platonic peck on his cheek. "Thank you, I guess," he said. "I would go to lunch with you, but we're very busy here. Very busy."

"I know. Please let me know if I can be of any help. I'm so

proud of you, Spencer. Bringing top cops to Cannes is a huge accomplishment. We are so lucky to have you here. You are a law enforcement treasure."

He cocked his head to the side and squinted, as if he was having a hard time seeing me. It was all I could do not to slap him.

"Are you ready, Bridget dear?" I asked.

"Are we leaving?"

"Time for lunch," I said sweetly and helped her up from her chair.

Fred appeared from the processing room, and his gloves were gone. His face was dripping sweat. "Thirty items," he said, out of breath. "Thirty. I feel sick. I'm seeing stars. I'm seeing my dead grandma. Grandma, I'm coming to you! Yes, Grandma, I'd love some pie!"

"Pie sounds good," I said to Bridget.

"I hear that Saladz has some great pear pie a la mode. I love mode," Bridget said.

"Let's get a lot of mode," I said. "I'll let you handle Fred and the conference," I told Spencer. "I'm sure you'll be able to handle it beautifully."

I sort of skipped to the door and turned around. I waved goodbye with my fingers, and I might have said toodle-oo.

Outside, my face dropped and I scowled, much to my

face's relief.

"Are you okay, Gladie?" Bridget asked. "You said some loopy things in there."

"Spencer didn't even apologize," I said, stomping toward Bridget's car. "The lying weasel."

"That woman is a big lie," Bridget agreed. "A D cup lie. A really pretty lie."

"I wonder if I would get arrested if I drowned him in the bathtub," I mused.

"Does this mean we're not going to eat pie a la mode?"

"I'm going to eat an *entire* pie a la mode. I'm going to eat all the mode in the world."

I didn't eat all of the mode, but I came pretty close. At Saladz, Bridget and I both ordered the Cobb salad and pear pie with three scoops of vanilla ice cream. Then, she had to get back to tax season, and I walked home.

We were having a gorgeous early spring, and there were wildflowers everywhere, just like the tourists. I welcomed the walk, since my belly was ready to burst, and the moment alone gave me time to think. I wasn't angry at Spencer, I realized, but there was a big lump of worry that was eating its way through me.

Worry.

It was worse than jealousy. It was the fear of losing Spencer, which was weird because I wasn't sure I wanted to keep him.

Yes, I loved him, but forever was a long time. I wasn't good with forever. I had only become good with two months, and forever was a lot longer than two months.

I swallowed, willing the worry to disappear, but it was wedged in my heart, and it refused to budge.

Damn it.

Love sucked donkey balls.

I reached my grandmother's house in about ten minutes. The house across the street was still selfie-central. Grandma's house was pretty busy, too, which was normal. Not only did she have daily classes and a steady stream of clients, but it was the center of activity for every Cannes organization. The driveway was packed with cars, and I squeezed between them to get to the front door.

"Daffodils!" I heard someone shout as I opened the door.

"Now, Morris," I heard my grandmother say calmly. "I'm sure we can come to a solution that will make everyone happy."

Inside, there were about a dozen people in the parlor, some on folding chairs and the others on the couches. I recognized most of them. I waved to Meryl, the blue-haired librarian, and she waved back. Morris was the head of the Daffodil Committee, and since we were in the middle of daffodil season, tensions were high. Not only was half of the town blooming with daffodils in front of every house and building, but the Daffodil Competition was coming up, and from what I had heard, it was dog-eat-dog to the blue ribbon and twenty-five-dollar gift card award to the local nursery.

Not wanting to take part of whatever daffodil drama was going on, I tiptoed away, but Morris called me back in.

"What do you think, Gladie?"

I stopped in my tracks and pointed at myself. "Me? I don't know much about flowers."

"Daffodils," one of the other committee members corrected. "Not regular flowers. Cannes is known for its March and April daffodil bloom. It's very important. Zelda, haven't you explained to your granddaughter about the importance of daffodils?"

"Gladie is very busy making love matches," she said, coming to my rescue, but the woman harrumphed and adjusted herself on her seat.

"Gladie, this town has been known for its yellow daffodils since the beginning of time," Morris told me. "Now these young upstarts," he continued, pointing to the ancient group of geriatrics. "want to do a white daffodil display at the Cannes Daffodil Competition. White, Gladie. White."

"White," some of the committee members said, tsking

loudly.

"Well…" I started, but my grandmother shook her head, warning me off giving my opinion. Actually, I had no opinion. White or yellow…what did I care?

Luckily, one of the women stood up and interrupted me. "Get with the times, Morris! White daffodils! White!"

He pointed at her, dramatically with his arm outstretched. "Heretic. Barbarian. Jezebel."

Grandma stood. "Now, now, Morris. Let's not get personal." Behind her back, my grandmother waved at me, signaling me to escape while I could. I took the hint and got out of the room and made my way to the kitchen.

Sanctuary.

It was just me, the linoleum floor, the Formica counters, and the seventy-year old appliances, table, and chairs. I made a pot of coffee and took a mug out of the cabinet. I opened the refrigerator and stuck my head inside it.

"You need to be careful, Gladie," I heard and turned around with the milk in my hand. Meryl had come into the kitchen, and she filled my mug with coffee and brought it to her lips.

"I don't know about daffodils," I said. "I tried to stay out of it."

She swatted the air. "Not that. Larry Doughy, your new match."

I took another mug out of the cabinet and filled it with coffee and milk. "Wow, news spreads like wildfire in this town. What about Larry? I know he's a little odd."

Meryl brought the cookie jar to the table and sat down. "He's cursed, not odd. A week ago, he was straight as an arrow. A log cabin Republican. He came into the library every Thursday to check out a new book on investment banking. Then, it all went to hell, and that man's cursed. If I were you, I'd stay far away from him."

I sat down and took a sip of my coffee. "Meryl, come on."

"Did you hear what happened to his foot?"

"No, but I saw his foot. I think he's just having a run of bad luck."

Meryl snorted. "Well, you can't say I didn't warn you."

"Thank you, Meryl. I don't believe in curses."

"Neither did I until Larry Doughy. That poor shlub is *cursed*." She put emphasis on the last word, and it sent a wave of anxiety up my spine. Could she be right? Could Larry Doughy be cursed?

Meryl grabbed a couple more cookies and went back to her daffodil meeting. I looked at the cookie jar and wondered if I should add them to the pie a la mode, which was digesting slowly in my stomach.

A scent of familiar, expensive cologne wafted up my nose, and Spencer walked into the kitchen. He plopped down on the chair next to me and slapped a battered bouquet of white daffodils onto the table.

"They were nice when I came in, but I was attacked when I walked past the parlor," he explained. "Crazy-ass town. Anyway, they're apology flowers. Gladie? Are you not talking to me?"

I felt myself blush, so I kept my gaze fixed on my cup of coffee.

"I'm sorry I wasn't totally honest with you," he continued. He had the nicest voice. It was deep and all male. It reminded me of when he spoke to me in bed at night, cradling me in his arms while he made love to me.

I couldn't help it. I looked up at him. We locked eyes, and he arched an eyebrow. "She's a hardass cop. Very competent, from Los Angeles. You know that I'm trying to make the Cannes police force halfway decent. It's not easy. I have to recruit good talent."

I nodded. Except for Remington, Spencer had to work with the Keystone Cops, and he hated it.

"For example, we had to call in the paramedics for Fred today because he has butt trauma. I mean, his butt is fine, but he was traumatized by a butt. How many police chiefs in this country have to deal with their desk sergeant having butt trauma?"

"I'm guessing not a whole lot," I said.

Spencer smiled. "There's my girl. I was worried I lost you."

"You're lucky you have me. Any other woman would have killed you."

He ran the back of his finger along my jawline. "I'm a very lucky man. Very lucky. Speaking of lucky, I've got some time. How about I get more lucky?"

"Your detective looks like Angelina Jolie."

"A young Angelina Jolie with bigger boobs and longer legs."

I sighed.

"Not that I noticed," he continued.

"Don't you need to be at work, preparing for the conference?"

"Oh, Pinky. After your visit today? Your English accent? When will you start to understand me?"

Spencer stood and pulled me up. He slipped his arms around me, crushing me against him. Then, he walked me to the wall and lifted me, wrapping my legs around his waist.

"The Daffodil Committee," I began.

"They're in there for thirty minutes more, at least. I need

five."

"Five minutes isn't the best sales pitch, Spencer. I don't care that you'll be satisfied in five minutes."

His fingers reached between my legs and began to caress me through my pants. "Who talked about me? This is all you, Pinky. Give me five minutes, and I'll give you ecstasy."

"Big talker," I said, but Spencer backed up his words with deft fingers and deep kisses. True to his word, I climaxed in four minutes, and he quieted my cries of ecstasy with his mouth on mine.

The Daffodil Committee were none the wiser.

CHAPTER 3

No matter what, no matter how much they don't want to, no matter how little they're enthusiastic about a date, make sure your matches always put their best foot forward. This isn't always easy to do, bubbeleh. A lot of people put their worst foot forward or only half of their best foot forward. You understand what I'm saying? Their best foot means that they dress nicely, brush their teeth, smile, and think of nice things to say over guacamole before the meal. It doesn't sound like much, but you'd be surprised at how much of a pain in the tuchus it is for many people. Naches to you, dolly, if you can get your matches to do their best. In other words, do your best to get your matches to do their best and love has got a shot. If you don't and they don't, they're shit out of luck.

Lesson 66, Matchmaking advice from your
Grandma Zelda

I woke up with Spencer kissing my nakedness from my naked upper half to my naked lower half. It was the best way to wake up, even better than breakfast in bed, although breakfast in bed sounded good, too.

"It's conference day," I moaned.

"Lift your knees up."

"You've got people coming in forty-five minutes."

"Pinky, let's work on us coming first, and then we'll worry about the conference."

Mitchell Shaw, who Grandma had matched with a retired foot model, delivered breakfast to the house as a thank you for finding him love, and it was ready on the table when I went downstairs after my quick shower with Spencer.

"This is called grits, dolly," Grandma said, holding up a bowl. "And this is country ham. That's different from regular ham, according to Mitchell. There's a whole world of food out there that I knew nothing about. Isn't that amazing? Live and learn."

Spencer ran in, adjusting his tie. "Oh my God. What's this? Look at those pancakes." He checked his watch. "I've got twelve minutes."

He sat down and piled food on his plate. "Zelda, this is great. You should get more clients who can cook."

"I like cooking matches, but even non-cooking ones seem to like to give me food," Grandma said, scooping grits onto her plate. "I haven't been hungry in sixty years."

"I've had to add five more miles to my daily run since I've started to eat here," Spencer said with his mouth full of pancakes and country ham. He pointed his fork at me. "Speaking of food, you're coming to lunch, right, Pinky?"

The conference was going to be a series of lectures, discussions, and social events. The night before, I was thrilled that Spencer actually invited me to participate in some of the social events. Normally, he insisted that I stay far away from his work, but since nobody had been murdered, I guessed it was okay.

Either that, or Spencer was feeling guilty.

I gnawed at the inside of my cheek, worrying about what Spencer felt guilty about.

After breakfast, it took me two hours to get ready for the law enforcement conference lunch. Grooming to show up the most beautiful woman in the world, who I was jealous of, was so much harder than grooming for a man or grooming for self-respect. Instead of looking good, I had to look good without looking like I was trying to look good so that Detective Hotsy Totsy would think that I always looked this good, and since she already saw me looking just so-so with chocolate-flavored lip balm, I had to look extra good without looking like I was trying to look extra good to make her forget about me looking so-so with chocolate-flavored lip balm.

Phew. Being jealous was exhausting.

By the time I was done, I was wearing a sheath dress, which was a size too small and strangled my body in such a way that I looked like Sophia Loren and made my c-cups look like double-Ds. Sure, I had grits and country ham working their way up my squeezed esophagus, but it was worth it. I practiced walking in my four-inch heels, and I applied another coat of base on my face like I was spackling a hole in the wall.

I took one more look at myself in the mirror. There. I was perfect. I was as hot as I could get and not get arrested for indecent exposure.

Take that, Detective Bitch Lady.

I changed purses into a small one with a spaghetti strap and walked slowly down the stairs, gripping the handrail for dear life so I wouldn't trip over my nosebleed shoes and fall to my death.

There was a frantic knock on the door, and Grandma went to get it. "Hold on with both hands, dolly," she told me as she passed. I held on, tighter and slowed my pace even more. "Coming," Grandma sang.

She opened the door, and I was surprised to see my new client, Larry Doughy. Uh oh. With all of the worrying over my competition, I hadn't started to find a match for Larry.

Grandma shot me a look that said everything. She would never have let a match down. She was constantly searching for love matches. Meanwhile, I was spackling my face.

"Larry," I said, brightly. "What can I do for you?"

"I'm cursed. I'm cursed," he said. He looked like a terrorized man. His hair was standing on end, and any remnants of a tie were long gone. "Uncurse me, now. Please."

"You're not cursed, Larry," I said, finally reaching the door.

"Maybe a little cursed," Grandma said, surprising me. I checked her face to see if she was joking, but she was dead serious.

"Will you give us a minute?" I asked Larry.

"Okay, but this house is structurally sound, right?" He asked, studying the doorframe.

"It'll be here until 2096," my grandmother told him with certainty. That seemed to mollify Larry.

I pulled my grandmother aside and whispered in her ear. "Is Larry really cursed?"

"Larry believes he's cursed. That's enough to curse him," she whispered back.

"What do I do?"

She put her hand on my shoulder and gave it a little

squeeze. "You know what to do, bubbeleh."

"Uh…" I said. I had no idea what to do. I didn't have the eensiest, beensiest idea what to do. I knew how to build a nuclear weapon more than I knew what to do with Larry Doughy and his curse. But since I often had no idea what to do in any given situation, I had this covered.

"Larry," I sang, like I was the hostess at a high-end spa, and he was a techie billionaire who wanted to lose twenty pounds in a weekend. I took his hands in mine. "I've been thinking nonstop about your problem, and I think I'm very close to a solution."

His face lifted with a burst of hope.

"You are?" he asked.

"I sure am." I was so going to hell. I was evil incarnate. I was worse than Detective Hot Body Witch. Actually, I wasn't that bad, but I was pretty bad.

"I'm so relieved, because I don't think I can handle having my house flooded again. Once this week was enough."

"It hasn't rained in two weeks," I said.

"I know."

"Well, I have to get going," I said. "I have a lunch at the police station to get to."

"I'll take you, and you tell me about your plan on the

way," he said.

I had run out of excuses about why Larry shouldn't drive me to the police station. He had a counter-argument for everything I came up with. In the end, time was ticking away, and I felt guilty. The man was obviously hurting. The very least I could do was to talk to him for the ten minutes it took to drive to the station.

"I heard about a woman who does a ritual with goats that's guaranteed to remove curses," he told me, driving away from the house.

A goat ritual sounded perfect. That way, I wouldn't have to think of my own way to get rid of his curse. "That's what I was thinking of. Remind me of her name, again. Turn left here."

"Moses Rathbone," he said, and I willed myself to remember the name. "I heard she treated John Travolta, and then he got *Pulp Fiction*."

We drove outside of the Historic District. "I'll get right on it, and I'm sure you'll be uncursed very soon and will find love, too." Come to think of it, I had better get him uncursed on the double because no woman wanted a man who needed goat rituals.

Larry honked his horn. "People don't know how to drive trucks," he said. Ahead of us was a large truck, and Larry was trying to get around him. I pulled the visor down and looked at myself in the mirror. We were two minutes away from the police station, and

I was getting nervous. I wanted to make a big entrance. I wanted to be noticed and make a statement. I wanted to show Spencer that I was something special, more special than Detective Snooty Bitch.

But I looked good. I was completely put together and ready to be the hostess with the mostess to Spencer's guests. I put the visor back in place. Larry honked the horn again and revved the motor.

"Bastard is blocking me," he grumbled.

"That's okay. The police station is up here. See it?"

The truck slowed down to a crawl, and Larry got around it and began to park in front of the police station. Outside in front of the station building, I could see Spencer with a group of people dressed in business attire. I assumed they were the top cops there for the conference.

"Thank you for the ride," I told Larry. "I'll call you in the next couple days to discuss the uncursing and possible matches."

"Do it quick before it gets worse."

I put my hand on his arm, reassuringly. "I'm certain you're going to be fine. I'm going to make sure of it."

The truck that we had been following crawled to a stop in front of us, its brakes screeching in protest. It sort of died there, parked at an angle. There was an explosion when it backfired. To my right, the top cops jumped in fear, and Detective Quick Draw Supermodel drew her gun and pointed it at the truck. The truck driver tried to start it again and ground the ignition. He pushed on the gas hard, and the truck roared to life, its tires screeching on the pavement as the truck shot forward.

"I'm sorry," Larry said to me.

"For what?"

"Wait for it."

I didn't have to wait for long. The truck lurched forward with surprising speed and quickly it lost control, swerving to the right, clipping the front of Larry's car. The back doors of the truck flung open, and its contents came flying out.

"This is going to be bad," Larry moaned.

I couldn't believe what I was seeing. The truck was filled with huge aquariums, but they weren't the fish kind of aquariums. They were the *oh my God* kind of aquariums. They flew out of the truck like projectiles, and I covered my head with my arms. The inhabitants of the aquariums slithered in the air and rained down on Larry's car, denting the hood and the roof and cracking the glass.

It was like a scene out of a horror movie. The world's scariest horror movie. A horror movie that stayed with you for years in your nightmares, giving you a lifetime of phobias and making you scream in terror at random times for no apparent reason.

"Snakes!" I shouted. "Snakes!"

"Snakes," Larry moaned. "I hate snakes. Why did it have to be snakes? Why couldn't it have been grenades? Grenades would have been better."

There were thousands of them. Millions of them. Bazillions of them. It was like every snake in the world was attacking the car. I didn't like snakes. I didn't even like worms. Now, I was being buried alive by snakes.

Buried alive by snakes!

Being buried alive was right up at the top of my list of biggest fears, but being buried alive by snakes blew my list to smithereens. It was like a torture chamber-Gladie-nightmare sandwich.

The deluge of slithering snakes seemed to last forever. It was a nonstop onslaught of gross. I screamed through all of it, my voice indefatigable. I was an opera diva scream queen, capable of holding a scream for hours. At least it seemed like hours. As I screamed, I watched in horror as the crack in the windshield grew longer and as the light dimmed, because the snakes blocked the windows.

Holy hell.

I screamed and screamed, but my screaming didn't help at all. The snakes kept coming. I grabbed onto Larry and shook him, turning my screaming toward him.

"Cursed. Cursed, cursed, cursed, cursed, cursed," he moaned, his eyes unblinking. I screamed in answer to him. I couldn't find any words, only screaming.

Finally, finally, like waiting for Christmas for ten years straight before it actually arrived kind of finally, it stopped. Some of the snakes slipped down to the hood and down to the ground, leaving only a few dozen tenacious reptiles on the car.

I was still scared out of my wits, but I stopped screaming.

Spencer knocked on my door window. "Don't open the door!" I shouted at him. "Don't open it! Snakes! Snakes! Oh, God! Snakes!"

"It's okay," he said through the closed window. "I'll make sure you don't touch a snake."

"No!" I shouted and held onto the door handle for dear life. "Don't open the door until all the snakes are gone!"

It took animal control forty-five minutes to clear away the snakes. The paramedics took Larry to the hospital for possible catatonia, and I finally allowed Spencer to open my door. As soon as it was open, I jumped out and onto his back, in order to avoid any possible straggler snakes that animal control missed. I wrapped my arms tight around his neck and my legs around his waist, but because my dress was a size too small, it couldn't take the added stress.

My dress ripped straight up from the hem, tearing the dress into two. The two pieces of material waved in the wind, as Spencer spun around, tugging at my hands around his neck to try to get air.

"Damn, that's a fine ass," one of the top cops announced.

Yep, I had made an entrance.

Spencer had bruises on his neck. I was wearing an orange jail jumpsuit because the only women's uniform they had for me to borrow was Detective Skinny Bitch's, and of course it didn't fit me. The lunch at the station had been kept warm by the caterer, thankfully, as the five top cops for the conference oohed and aahed about our town's phenomenal first responders. That was lucky for me because Spencer wasn't furious at me for fouling up day one of his conference.

Our table for lunch was set in the station's conference room. There were seven of us, a caterer, and a server. Spencer sat between two super cops, and I was relegated to a seat on the other side of the table. The centerpiece was a huge bouquet of yellow daffodils.

I slumped down in my seat and tugged at my jumpsuit collar, humiliated. In the action, my hair had turned into a frizzball, and I had screamed off a bunch of my makeup. I didn't look like I had planned. I was making an impression, but it wasn't the one I wanted.

Spencer stood and clinked his glass with a spoon. "I want to formally thank you all for coming to Cannes to attend this conference. It's a small conference in a small town, but that doesn't mean it isn't important. I firmly believe that together we can come up with recommendations to improve law enforcement policies and procedures throughout Southern California."

"Here. Here," the man to my right said. He had been introduced to me as Sidney Martin, a retired police lieutenant from Long Beach. Sidney was dressed like a penguin. In fact, everything about him reminded me of a bird. His lips were pursed like a beak and he was perfectly dressed and groomed in a three-piece suit, like he had pristine plumage. I figured he was in his early sixties.

In my orange jumpsuit, I was definitely self-conscious next to his dapperness, but I was a step up from Captain Leah Wilder on my other side, who was dressed in a shlumpy skirt and blouse with a gray, long, droopy cardigan, which mirrored her long, droopy face and gray hair.

"I'm so sorry that you had such a bad experience," she said to me sweetly after Spencer sat down, and we were served the salad.

"It wasn't that bad," I lied. In fact, I couldn't think of anything worse. Thank goodness there was wine at lunch, but I didn't think any amount of chardonnay was going to erase the vision of snakes coming at me like bullets from a machine gun every time I closed my eyes.

"I've been in law enforcement since I was nineteen, and I've never seen anything like that," Leah continued.

The man sitting across from us snorted and chewed his lettuce with his mouth open. "Snakes. Big deal," he said, spitting out a piece of lettuce, which landed on the table next to my glass. He was top cop Mike Chantage, from Los Angeles. I didn't know his exact title, but it was obvious that he was in a high position. "Snakes are nothing compared to the things I've seen on the job," he sneered. "If you work hard, you see more than snakes."

Leah crumpled her napkin and threw it on the table next to her salad bowl, as if she were upset that Mike had seen more than snakes in his work.

"Please excuse Mike," Leah told me. "He's old school, but as I'll explain to the group during the conference, I'm an expert on new law enforcement that I think will bring on better results and a better quality of life for everyone if they're implemented."

"What the hell do we care about a better quality of life?" the man sitting next to Spencer roared. "We're cops. Cops. We're not social workers. There's nothing better than meeting force with force. Anything else is BS." He was Frank Fellows, and he looked like he had swallowed enough steroids to make a second person in his skin. His muscles bulged everywhere, like a grotesque version of Arnold Schwarzenegger.

"Big talker," Mike sneered and picked up his salad bowl and looked around. "I'm ready for the second course," he called.

The waiter jogged over to him and took his bowl. Then he collected the rest of the bowls, and the caterer spooned our main course onto plates. He looked familiar, but I couldn't place him.

Then, I did.

The caterer was the survivor from the plane crash. Arthur Fox. The last time I had seen him, he was hopping out of the wreckage, his skin blackened from smoke and covered in cuts and scrapes. I knew that he had decided to stay in the town he had crashed in. I also knew that he had no family and had acquired a superstitious attachment to Cannes for its power to save his life. I silently prayed that he wouldn't recognize me. I was already the snake lady; I didn't want them to think of me as the plane crash lady, too.

The second course was salmon, mashed potatoes, and asparagus. It was fancy fare for a police station, and it reminded me that this conference was very important to Spencer. I tried to push back my snake trauma and forget that I was wearing an orange jumpsuit and tried to make Spencer proud of my cosmopolitan charm and sophistication.

As we ate, I acted as a tour guide, giving the top cops thrilling accounts of the plethora of pie shops and antique places in Cannes. "My wife would have liked to do some shopping here," the muscly Frank said.

"That's not all she likes," Mike chuckled with his mouth full of potatoes.

There was a stunned silence at the table, and Spencer and I exchanged looks. There was always one rotten apple in the bunch, and this bunch of top cops might have a couple bad apples. Spencer reached down and pulled out a file folder.

"Here's the rundown of our scheduled events for the conference. This afternoon and tomorrow is back-to-back presentations and discussions, but I'm sure you'll be able to squeeze in some time after, if you'd like to do some sightseeing or shopping. The day after tomorrow, we're planning on doing some field work experimentation, as we've discussed."

He passed around the paper, and the participants looked it over while their plates were cleared.

"There's a mistake here," Joyce Strauss said, looking down her nose at the paper. She looked down her nose at everything and everybody. It wasn't that she was tall, but just that she thought she knew more than any other human, and maybe she did. She was painfully thin, as if eating was beneath her, too. "I'm supposed to speak first. I'm sure that was made clear in the planning of the conference."

Spencer read the paper. "Were you? I guess that was a mistake."

"Obviously," she said. She pulled a thick red marker out of her purse and slashed through the schedule, marking it with arrows. "There. I've fixed it. And I've fixed other mistakes I found, too. It'll run more smoothly, now."

There was a general buzzing of indignation around the table, as everyone worried about the placement of their talks and how much time they would be given, now that Joyce had changed everything.

Joyce clapped her hands together, like an old-fashioned school marm. "This is all very simple. Chief Bolton, allow me to take the reins, and I'll make sure the conference runs smoothly."

I gulped down the rest of my wine and snuck out to the bathroom. I didn't want to stick around to see Spencer get bent out of shape with the threat of Joyce Strauss messing up his hard work and planning. It wasn't easy to corral five top cops with top egos. I didn't envy him.

I heard footsteps behind me. Sidney Martin, the birdlike man, was shuffling quickly toward me in the hall. "I wanted to get out of there, too," he said, smiling with his pursed lips.

"I just had to wash my hands," I said.

"Perhaps you could point me in the direction of the men's room? I'm actually making an exit so I don't have to eat the dessert. I like to cook my own meals, you see, and I have a sensitive palate. Not that the catering wasn't bad, but it's not what I'm used to."

"You cook?" I asked. Men who cooked were a rare commodity. The idea made my skin prickle with excitement, and I realized it was important. Why was it important that he could cook? Then, I remembered. My new client Cynthia wanted a man who could cook. And what else? Oh, yes. A full head of hair. I studied Sidney's hair. It looked pretty thick to me. Then, I looked at his hands. No rings.

Bingo.

I had found a possible match for Cynthia without trying. I loved when work entailed little or no actual work. It almost made up for my other client, Larry Doughy and his curse. Almost.

I came up with a plan quickly to make the match. I'd have

to make an excuse to crash Spencer's conference again and bring Cynthia to do some matchmaking. It was a perfect way for a no-pressure first meeting.

"The bathroom is second door on the left," I told Sidney. He shuffled past me. The ladies bathroom was in the other direction. On my way, I heard Detective Terri's voice, and I cowardly hid in the supply closet. I didn't want any one-on-one face time with her while she was the most beautiful woman in the world, and I was in my post-snake trauma and orange jumpsuit. I closed myself into the closet and put my ear up against the door. It must have been made out of balsa, because I could hear every word.

She was berating Fred again. Sure, Fred probably deserved a lot of berating, but he was my first match, and he liked me, and I felt protective over him.

Also, I hated Detective Bitchy Hot Stuff.

"Don't make me tell you again," she ordered. "Process the perp and make it snappy."

Make it snappy. She sounded like an Irish cop in the 1920s. She should have at least said, please. Didn't she know that she could get more flies with honey?

"But I'm the desk sergeant. I don't do processing..." Fred moaned.

I wanted to jump out of the closet and tell her to leave Fred alone. But I was a coward. I was a cowardly coward from Coward Town. I was yellow. I was chicken. I was spineless. I was a namby-pamby, pantywaist fraidy cat who didn't want to take on an armed beauty with a bad attitude who could probably put me in a chokehold before I could pull up the orange pants part of my orange jumpsuit and give her a taste of my Krav Maga skills that I had gotten during a buy one lesson get one free Groupon special…nonexistent skills, come to think of it, because I had stopped for chili cheese fries on the way to class and never actually got there or learned any Krav or Maga.

Damn it. I was a terrible defender. I needed a dragon. A dragon could have really come in handy.

Oh, lord. I was getting a warped sense of reality since Spencer had ordered the premium channels for my bedroom television.

But a dragon really would have come in handy.

I heard Fred and Detective Meaner Than Spit walk down the hallway. I opened the closet door a crack and peeked out. The coast was clear. I tiptoed back to the conference room, but suddenly Fred was there walking with a man in handcuffs.

"You don't have things up your butt, do you?" Fred asked him.

"Define 'things'," the man said.

My cellphone rang, and I dug it out of my purse and answered it. It was my grandmother.

"Get home fast, dolly," she said. "Goats."

CHAPTER 4

It's not if you win or lose, it's how you play the game. Have you heard that, bubbeleh? What do you think about that? You think it doesn't matter how you make a match, it's only important if you make a match? You could be right! How do I know? Actually, I do know, and I'll tell you how I know. I'm in the love business, dolly, and I do this for love. So do you. Make a match on a roof. Make a match through the mail. Be creative. Be boring. Make a match any way you want. But only make a match through love. Bring love to the matchmaking, and the matchmaking will result in love. It's all about the love, dolly.

Lesson 91, Matchmaking advice from your
Grandma Zelda

Spencer had a patrol car take me home. My grandmother's house was still bustling, and the driveway was packed with cars, as was the street outside.

"I hope the Daffodil Committee isn't here," Officer James said, as he stopped in front of the house. "We've been out all day on calls of crazy people digging up daffodils and planting other colors. I mean, who cares about daffodils?"

I sure didn't, but they seemed to elicit a lot of emotion in Cannes residents. "How do you like the new detective?" I asked, shameless.

"Detective Williams? Finest looking woman I've ever seen outside of the JC Penney catalog, but she's a hardass. I don't mean her ass is hard. I mean, she's one scary female. I try to stay clear of her line of sight. Fred's on the front desk, so he can't hide from her, and she's got him looking up butts morning, noon, and night. It was nice seeing you, again, Underwear Girl."

"Nice seeing you, too," I said and opened my door.

I walked into the house to see a man in the entranceway, pointing at another. "Saboteur!" he shouted. "Saboteur!"

"Cool your jets. I didn't dig up your daffodils."

I side-stepped around them and found my grandmother. "I can't believe they're still here," I told her.

"Tell me about it. It's thrown a wrench into my Satisfying Singles workshop. Flowers are serious business, dolly."

"And there are goats, too?"

"The goat lady. Moses. The one who does the goat ritual. She says she's been hired to uncurse Larry Doughy. She's here to coordinate with you."

"I'm not sure I want to be in on a goat ritual. I don't have a lot of luck with animals, lately."

A woman in overalls, who smelled like a petting zoo, approached me. "Are you Burger?"

I nodded. "I'm Gladie Burger."

"Your man Larry wants to do this tonight, but the goat won't be ready until the day after tomorrow. Sundown. Does that work for you?"

No. It didn't work for me at all. And I didn't know what the goat ritual entailed or why the goat took two days to get ready. "I don't think Larry needs a goat ritual, but if he does, that's his thing, not mine. I'm a matchmaker."

I caught Grandma smiling at me, proud as punch, and it gave me courage.

"You're making a mistake," the goat woman warned me. "My goat has an eighty-two percent success rate, and your Larry has got a doozy of a curse on him. Did you hear about the snake thing?"

"I might have heard something about it," I said.

She leaned forward and looked me in the eye. "That's just

the start. He's got a creeper curse on him. You know what that means?"

"What does that mean?" one of the daffodil people asked. They had stopped fighting over flowers and were riveted to our goat conversation.

"A creeper curse means it creeps on the victim and grows," the goat woman explained.

"Grows how?" a daffodil woman asked behind me.

"Like weeds," the goat woman said. "Like mold. It's a shitstorm honker of a curse."

Everyone stared at me like I had cursed Larry Doughy myself. Then, there was a general clearing of throats and the Daffodil Committee began to file out on the double.

"You'll be calling me," the goat lady told me and left with the rest.

"You cleared them out," Grandma said to me, surprised at my gift for making people flee from me. "Thank you. It's been a helluva day. I'm going to make some cocoa and take a bath."

That sounded wonderful. "Me, too," I said.

I brought my cup of cocoa with four jumbo-sized marshmallows in it, plus the rest of the bag of marshmallows, to my bathroom. I turned on the water in my claw-footed bathtub and unfortunately caught my reflection in the mirror.

Orange wasn't my color. It made my skin look orange and blotchy, and my eyes had a weird glow, like I was a psychotic killer who had come back from the dead. The jumpsuit was baggy and made me look twenty-five pounds heavier. My hair had an electric shock thing happening, and what was left of my makeup had smeared down my cheeks.

I sighed and dug into the bag of jumbo marshmallows, sticking one into my mouth. I stepped out of the jumpsuit and brought the cocoa and bag of marshmallows with me as I stepped into the tub.

There's nothing better in the whole world that a deep bathtub filled with scalding hot water except for a deep bathtub filled with scalding hot water while drinking hot cocoa and eating jumbo-sized marshmallows.

I had it all.

Sure, now in addition to being the woman who had cursed a house, I was also the snake lady, and sure I had flashed all of Spencer's top cops and ruined the conference that he had been working on for weeks, and sure I couldn't compete with Detective Boobs and Legs on any level. But at least I was submerged in hot water and was eating jumbo-sized marshmallows. At least I had a lead on a match. At least my grandmother was ordering the pasta explosion buffet meal from Sal's Italian Eatery for dinner.

In the world of humiliations, I was a glass half-full kind of girl.

Once the bath was full, I turned off the water. I downed the cocoa quickly and put the cup on the floor. I got through three more jumbo marshmallows before I fell fast asleep.

I woke up when Spencer turned the water back on. "You're going to catch pneumonia, Pinky," he said, letting out the cold water and refilling it with hot. "That looks good, especially with you in it. What's floating on top?"

"Jumbo-sized marshmallows."

"Pinky, you never cease to amaze me. Jumbo-sized marshmallows? Damn if you're not the sexiest woman alive."

His words said marshmallows, but his eyes were looking elsewhere in the bathtub. I watched him strip down and drop his clothes onto the tile floor. He turned off the water, stepped into the tub, and sat down, facing me.

"I like how your boobs float in the water," he said, ogling my breasts.

"Aren't you supposed to be at your conference?"

"Ugh. Why didn't you stop me from hosting a conference, Pinky? What a bunch of turds. Since they wanted to alter the schedule, I included a free evening for them and got the hell out of there."

"I'm sorry Joyce Strauss did that to you," I said, as Spencer took my foot and touched it to his how-do-you-do.

"She wasn't so bad, but that Mike Chantage is a piece of work. I don't know what the story is there, but he's putting everyone in a bad mood, including me. He told Terri that I was cutting corners."

The hair on the back of my neck stood up, but I didn't know why. "What does that mean? Like stealing?"

"Something like that. Not doing things by the book. And Pinky, besides all of your shenanigans with my cases, I've done everything by the book."

"Shenanigans?" I said, affronted. I pulled my foot back, but Spencer got hold of my arms and pulled me on top of him.

"Where do you think you're going?" he demanded and cupped my ass with his strong hands.

"Wherever you're going, I'm assuming," I said and settled in for sex in the bathtub, which was even better than marshmallows in the bathtub.

Spencer's face was rough with stubble, but his lips were soft. He kissed me with a particular urgency, as if he was trying to prove something or trying to erase the rest of the world. I didn't mind erasing the rest of the world because the here and now of the two of us naked, aroused, and touching was all that I needed.

He lifted me up onto him until he was nestled inside me. I began to move against him, a familiar rhythm we had together, while his fingers touched me in just the right place.

Our weeks together of desperate need, in which we attacked each other like it was all going to evaporate into thin air, had settled into a glorious habit of coming together, of communication on a whole different level between two people who wanted to be one. Making love is what the romance authors would call it, and they would be right. There was a scary intensity to it, but funnily enough, I wasn't scared at all when I was in Spencer's arms.

No, the fear came later, when he was Spencer again, and I was Gladie and "we" returned to "he" and "I."

But in any case, my day had definitely taken a turn for the better.

"This pasta explosion is just what the doctor ordered," Spencer said, scooping rigatoni off his plate and shoveling it in his mouth.

Grandma was wearing her housedress, Spencer was wearing a robe, and I was wearing Spencer's sweats and t-shirt. The dinner had arrived right on time, but Spencer hadn't stopped complaining about his conference's participants.

"That son of a bitch Mike Chantage. If I can find a way to lock him in the holding cell for the rest of the conference, I'm going to do it. Little bastard. And what's with Frank Fellows? I've never seen a grown man pout as much as him. He just stares at Mike and pouts. Not as much as Leah. She's a sweet thing, but it's like her head spins around when she's near Mike. Mike. Mike, Mike, Mike. I checked him out, again, just to make sure I hadn't made a mistake with him, but his credentials are stellar, and his references pristine. Are there any more breadsticks?"

I passed him the breadsticks.

"Did you clock him?" my grandmother asked me.

"Twenty-two minutes, according to the oven clock."

"Twenty-two minutes? What are you talking about?" Spencer asked.

"You've been complaining for twenty-two minutes," I explained.

"No, I haven't."

"It seemed like longer, sweetie pie," Grandma told Spencer.

He blushed ever so slightly. "Well, these people are a pain in the ass. Zelda, if you were in my shoes, you would be complaining, too."

"I don't doubt it," she said, sweetly.

"The best part of my day was the snakes," he continued, and then shot me a look and winked. "Well, the second-best part of my day."

"How do I look?" Cynthia asked me. She was wearing a wrap-around dress and flats. Her hair was ironed straight.

"You're going to knock his socks off," I told her, and I wasn't lying. She looked tidy and put together enough for the fastidious Sidney Martin.

"You're sure about the cooking?"

"Yep. And he's got hair."

Luckily for me, Spencer was already fed up with his conference, so I figured he wouldn't mind if I crashed it with a potential match.

I drove Cynthia to the station in my Oldsmobile Cutlass Supreme. This time, I parked in back and snuck in so I wouldn't have to see Detective Snooty Face. The conference room was darkened, and Frank Fellows was standing at the head of the room talking in front of a Power Point presentation. I pointed Cynthia to a seat next to Sidney, and I stood at the back of the room.

"That was 2012," Frank was saying. "The officer in question had lost his sense of smell in a boating accident but failed to inform the force. Two months later, he stopped a van and couldn't tell that it was jam packed with a half-ton of marijuana. Since his olfactory system was impotent, he missed the bust. He was promptly fired, and then he turned around and sued."

"Sucks to be impotent, doesn't it, Frank?" Mike called out

and sniggered.

Frank clenched his fists and took a step forward. "Don't do it, Frank," Leah said.

"I don't need you to defend me," Mike told her.

The tension in the group had escalated since the day before, and I didn't blame Spencer one bit for complaining about it.

Spencer thanked Frank for his talk. "Next up, Sidney Martin is going to tell us about the club that prison inmates had organized, with thousands of X-rated DVDs, alcohol, rubber gloves, and lubricants."

"That sounds fascinating," Cynthia gushed at Sidney, laying it on thick. He looked at her, startled. "Why did they want rubber gloves and lubricants?" she asked.

"Who the hell are you?" Spencer asked.

"This is Cynthia," I said. "She's very interested in law enforcement. She's a retired county clerk, and she has a pension and owns a split-level condo. She likes long walks at sunset, gourmet meals, and pets that don't shed. She's open to men of any religion or none at all. She likes to travel, but she also enjoys just staying home and watching television with a special someone. Totally single, Cynthia has never married, hoping to find that special someone who wants to share a life with her and enjoy the same interests."

I gulped air and smiled at Sidney. Cynthia was smiling at him, too. It had taken me fifteen minutes to memorize my Cynthia pitch, and it went off without a hitch. How could Sidney resist it?

"Pinky, what the hell are you doing here?" Spencer demanded. "And what the hell are you talking about? Hoping to find that special someone? Are you working?"

"Shut up," I said.

"I'm so confused," Leah said.

"I propose we have our lunch break before Sidney gives us the rundown on the prison club for masturbation," Joyce said in her high, pinched voice. Once again, she was bossing everyone around, but this time, Spencer seemed relieved.

"Good idea, Joyce," he said, but he was looking right at me. Cynthia, meanwhile, only had eyes for Sidney.

"I like your hairstyle," she was telling him.

"I have a standing appointment on Thursdays at Mel's Hair and Care," he told her.

Spencer scowled at me and pointed toward the door. I met him out in the hallway. He crowded me until my back was against the wall and he put his hand on the wall above my head. "Pinky, what are you up to?"

"You're always telling me to be a matchmaker and not get involved with murders. So, here I am. I'm matching Cynthia with

Sidney. They're perfect for each other."

"You're matching them at my conference?"

"Yes, aren't you proud of me? No dead people."

"But my conference."

"No dead people."

Spencer shut his eyes tight. "No dead people?"

"Scout's honor."

He opened his eyes. "Pinky, you were never a scout."

"No dead people. I promise."

Spencer had dreamy eyes, and he was targeting me with all of his dreaminess. "I guess if there's no dead people, it'll be okay. Oh, shit. What am I saying? You can't do matchmaking during my conference. This is my job."

I put my hands on my hips. "So what are you saying? Your job is worth more than mine? Your business is more important than mine? Is that where we stand in this relationship? You're the big, bad policeman so you're more important than I am? I just do love, and love isn't important? That's rich coming from the man who says he loves me. Does that mean that I shouldn't care about your loving me because love isn't a big deal? Huh? Huh? You should be ashamed of yourself, Spencer Bolton. Deeply ashamed. I expected a lot from you, but never this. Not discarding our love like it was nothing. Throwing away our relationship when we've just begun. I've given you the best two months of my life! I've devoted myself to you. And now this? This? Whoa to the woman who loves man because her heart will be broken."

I was running out of steam and running out of words. My goal was to confuse him or wear him out or simply make him fear for the future of his orgasms. Whatever I was doing, it was working. He was scared, upset, and worn out all at once.

"I didn't mean any of that, Pinky," he said in his seductive voice. "I meant...Okay, your match can stay. We're having lunch now, anyway. But no deaths."

I crossed my heart. "Cross my heart. No deaths."

The conference room was once again turned into a dining area. The caterer was back with a waiter, and this time, he recognized me.

"You're the woman who called the paramedics, right?" Arthur Fox asked me, as he decorated the room with daffodils. The conference participants were milling about, talking to each other. Even Mike was talking to others and smiling.

"I witnessed the crash, but emergency services came on their own," I said, not wanting to take credit for saving him. "How are you enjoying the town?"

"Love it. I couldn't have asked for a nicer welcome, despite the circumstances."

It was odd to move into the town that you literally crashed

into, but I did understand how Cannes could grow on a person.

"I'm happy that you're okay," I said.

"My leg hurts when it rains, but that's about it. A miracle."

"A miracle," I agreed, but I didn't want that to get around. It was one thing having a town believe that I could curse it, but it was another thing altogether for them to believe that I could do miracles. I wouldn't get a moment of rest.

Arthur Fox and the waiter laid out the table settings with the food. Chicken, rice, and vegetables. There was extra food, and Arthur gave Cynthia and me each a plate. Cynthia looked around the table and down at the food, and the color drained from her face.

"Excuse me," she said and stood. She went quickly toward the door, knocking into Mike. "Excuse me," she said again, this time to Mike, touching his shoulder and then left the room.

I locked eyes with Sidney, and I tried to read what he could have done to make Cynthia fly out of the room on the double, but he seemed as nonplussed as I was. The rest of the room was eating intently. This time, there was no toast and no conversation. The conference was a lot like dinner with my mother when I was a teenager. It started with conflict and ended in quiet passive aggressiveness. Whatever was going on in the law enforcement conference, I hoped that my match could be salvaged.

I folded my napkin and got up to find Cynthia and see how she was, but before I took a step, Mike Chantage coughed violently. Fear climbed up my spine, and I stopped in my tracks, my eyes riveted to Mike as he tried to catch his breath, as his body convulsed with deep, wracking coughs.

A flash of certainty passed through me. I knew what I was watching, and I knew what was going to happen. An image of Mike lying in a coffin flashed in my mind, and it was more real than the scene in front of me. I tried to catch Spencer's attention to let him know what was going to happen, but he was focused on Mike, and it looked like he had an inkling about what was about to happen, too.

Mike grabbed at his throat in a blind panic. His eyes were wild, darting from side to side, as the reality of not being able to breathe hit him. It was impotence. The real kind. The life or death kind.

"You did it," he croaked with his last breath. "You killed me."

His stomach complained loudly, and he threw up, spraying vomit over the table. Then, as a punctuation mark announcing the end of Mike's life, his eyes rolled up in his head, and he collapsed with a crash, face first on his plate of chicken.

Even with a table of top cops, there wasn't an immediate rise to action, probably because we were all in shock. Spencer was the first to act, flying from his seat to scoop Mike's head up and lay him gently on his back on the floor, where Spencer began to do CPR.

I could have told him it was no use, but I didn't know how

I knew it was no use. As Spencer did CPR, the others began to act. The paramedics were called, but nobody assisted Spencer with the CPR. Instead, they circled him, and watched as Spencer went to work. Ten minutes later, the paramedics took over, but it was no use.

Mike Chantage was dead.

CHAPTER 5

A matchmaker is a yenta. Nosy is our business. How else could we do what we do? But a matchmaker isn't a noodnik. In other words, we're curious. We listen. But we don't pester or bother. You get me, bubbeleh? As my good friend Roy Campanella told me once, it's better to watch and wait and let things happen. Be there to catch, if it's a strike or if it's a ball. Fast ball, curve, slider. It doesn't matter. Catch all of it, dolly. Don't let it get past you.

Lesson 25, Matchmaking advice from your
Grandma Zelda

"Sawasdee, Gladie. That means hello in Thai."

Lucy was Skyping me on my cellphone. She was smiling ear to ear, and she showed me her beautiful Thai outfit and the beach behind her. "I'm having the time of my life, darlin'," she gushed. "Nobody's happier than I am. This cruise is the best thing since Botox. Better, maybe. No, scratch that. Botox is pretty damned good. But it's better than fillers. A smidge too much filler, and you look like Boris Karloff. Where are you? You look like you're in a cave."

"I'm in interrogation room three," I said.

"Is that some kind of new kinky thing you're doing with Spencer? Lord, you two just started, and you've already run out of the regular stuff and have moved onto the kinky stuff?"

I shook my head. "No, we're still doing a lot of the regular stuff. I'm in the interrogation room at the police station, about to be interrogated by Detective Fuck Face Pretty Girl."

"Excuse me?"

I gave Lucy the rundown on Spencer's new hire.

"That little pisser," she complained. "He had no right. There are lines you don't cross, and he just up and crossed them. I'll have Harry get someone to break his thumbs."

Harry was her new husband, and he had contacts who knew how to break thumbs.

"Thank you," I said. "But I still need Spencer's thumbs."

There was nothing better than a friend agreeing with me about Spencer's mistreatment. It calmed me and made me feel better, immediately.

"That's not the worst thing," I said.

"You killed someone," she gasped.

"Shush! I didn't kill anyone. I just witnessed a death."

"Like always," Lucy said.

"No, usually I find them after they're already dead. This one died in front of me and in front of Spencer, the four cops at his conference, the caterer, and a waiter."

Lucy's smile vanished, and her face dropped. "Damn it. I miss everything. Here I am on this stupid-ass cruise, when I could be there. Idiotic honeymoons. I'm over here with boring room service, and you're watching people drop dead."

"I thought it was better than fillers."

"Bull hockey. I'm stuck on a boat most days, traveling to places I can't pronounce. You get all the fun."

"Lucy, it was bad. A man died. It's a tragedy."

"Yeah, yeah, whatever. So, who killed him? Have you figured it out, yet?"

"Nobody killed him. He just dropped dead onto his chicken. He wasn't in the best shape. He looked like a heart attack waiting to happen."

But that wasn't the whole truth. I left out the part about his last words: "You killed me." If I told Lucy about that, she would never let me off the phone.

"Gladie, why are you in interrogation room three?" Lucy asked, putting it all together.

"I'm a witness, and since Spencer was a witness, too, they're having Detective Thighmaster Meanie interrogate me."

"That bitch! I'm madder than a wet hen. How dare Spencer let that she-wolf interrogate you? I wish I was there, Gladie. I'd save you and whup that girl's ass."

I wished Lucy was there, too, and that she would whup her ass, but Detective Hardass had a gun and mace and would have Tased my friend before she got one southern insult out. Speaking of hardass, the door opened, and she walked in.

"Gotta go," I whispered into my phone and turned it off.

Detective Boner Machine was dressed in a simple black suit and work shoes with her hair pulled back in a ponytail, but she looked like a runway model. I smiled at her, remembering that I was supposed to be killing her with kindness and be above it all.

She didn't smile back.

"This is routine," she said and sat across from me. She held a pen poised over a yellow legal pad. "Name, address." I gave her my basic information. "Why were you at the scene?"

She locked eyes with me, and I could read her mind. She thought I was a whiny, clingy girlfriend who couldn't mind her own business. I straightened my back.

"I was here on business. I brought a client to meet someone."

"You're in business? What kind of business?"

"I'm a matchmaker," I said with every ounce of pride I could muster. There wasn't a lot of prestige with the matchmaker moniker, but at least it wasn't the beer drains cleaner at Hoboken Sports Arena, which I had done for six horrible days.

"A what? That's really a job?" she asked in her condescending, beautiful voice.

I smiled big, as if I thought she was interested in my work and thought it was cool. "Oh, yes. I work with my grandmother. She's famous in this town. We've made a lot of very happy couples. I would be more than happy to help you find a match as a welcome to Cannes gift," I said sweetly.

She narrowed her eyes. "I can find my own man. I don't need a creepy matchmaker to fix me up."

I willed myself to keep smiling. At some point, I figured, she was going to succumb to my charms and like me. But for now, she hated my guts, and I didn't know why. "Of course," I said. "I didn't mean to imply otherwise. So, you have your eye on someone?"

"Not that it's your business, but I guess you should know that yes, I have my eye on someone I work with."

A quiet descended on the room, like a Mac truck ramming the back of the car you're driving. *Boom.* Whiplash. My smile vanished and reappeared on Detective Danger's face, as if she had stolen it from my face.

I would have bet money that it wasn't the only thing that she wanted to steal.

And who wouldn't want to steal Spencer? He was gorgeous and smart and funny and chief of police. Sure, he was a frat boy who likes *Family Guy* reruns and way too much baseball, but that was small potatoes in all things annoying compared to other men out there.

Spencer was mine, but he was just a man, and Detective Hotness McBitchyface was more than a woman. I doubted she had ever been rejected in her life, and I didn't hold out much hope that Spencer would be the first man on the planet to tell her no.

Her intent was clear, and she wanted me to know all about it. At that moment, I searched my memory for my grandmother's advice. What would Zelda do? I wished I could call her and ask, but I didn't think I was going to get a telephone break.

I had to rely on my wits.

Damn it. I wasn't great in the wits department.

I sat up straighter in my seat and made my mouth turn up in a smile, again. "I'm so happy for you, Detective. Love makes life so much sweeter."

"Whatever." She looked down at her notes. "Obviously, Mike had a massive heart attack. The man probably hadn't seen the inside of a gym in years, and he sucked down chips and dip like a junkie getting his fix. So, it was just a matter of time."

Beads of sweat popped out on my forehead. I hadn't seen the inside of a gym in years, either, and I sucked down chips and dip whenever they were in arm's distance. Now I was worried that I was going to pass out dead on a chicken breast, just like Mike.

"You're probably right," I said. "But he did say…"

"I know what he said. Do you think you're the first one I'm interviewing, Ms. Burger? You think you're that important? You think I'm dying to pick your brain because you're so perceptive? Believe me, this is routine. Every question in this with you is routine. I do it because I'm a professional, not because I think you're all that. You're not all that. You're not even half that. Not even five percent that."

Holy cow. She really didn't like me.

And another holy cow. I really didn't like her.

"So, that's why I have to ask you this: Did you see anything out of the ordinary leading up to the passing?"

The passing? Well, everyone hated Mike. He had openly insulted every person in the conference, and Spencer couldn't stand him. There was also the little detail of his last words, which were that someone had killed him, and he knew the person in question.

"No, I didn't notice anything," I told her.

She tapped her pen against her legal pad. "Good. I've heard that you like to stick your nose into law enforcement business. That's changed as of now, do you understand me? No amateur sleuthing. No buttinski messing with my case."

She shot me her meanest, scariest cop face. I knew that face. I slept with that face every night. I wasn't scared of that face.

"Oh, of course, Detective," I said, sweetly. "I'm very busy, matching couples. I'm terribly sorry about Mike. What a tragedy. Please let me know if a memorial is planned and where I can send flowers." I looked at my naked wrist. "Oh, look at the time. I have an appointment that I must get to. Am I allowed to leave now?'

"Remember what I told you. Don't get involved."

"Of course not," I lied.

"Because I'm in charge. Do you understand? I'm in charge. Me. The chief picked *me*."

I willed my mouth to stay upturned in a broad smile. "Of course," I sang, like nothing made me happier.

Detective Ball Buster Beauty let me out of the interrogation room and escorted me out of the station, effectively giving me the boot. Outside, I called Cynthia to make sure she was all right, but it went right to voicemail. I texted her, but she didn't respond to that, either.

I needed coffee.

I drove to Tea Time. It turned out that I arrived during a rare moment when the tea shop was empty. I ordered a latte from Ruth and sat at a corner table by the bar. "You look like someone shot your puppy, Gladie."

She was close.

"One of the cops at Spencer's conference died."

"Aren't you used to that, already? Wherever you go, you trip over dead people. Frankly, with you coming in here all the time, I'm shocked as shit I'm still alive."

She was right. She should be shocked.

"You're wrong, Ruth. I walk all day long and don't trip over dead people. Normally. Not for weeks."

My phone rang. It was Lucy on Skype, again. "Well? Did they clap you in irons? Are you in solitary? Harry says we can fly home if you need me."

"What the hell are you talking about?" Ruth demanded, peeking over my shoulder.

"Did they get you too, Ruth?" Lucy asked.

"I'm at Tea Time, getting coffee," I explained. "They let me go. I'm not a suspect. They said the man dropped dead of a heart attack. He ate chips."

"If chips killed him, then, you're done for," Ruth told me.

"Put the phone closer to your face," Lucy said. She studied my face in close up. "Oh my God. You've got it bad. You're on the case. You're a dog with a bone. It's the Miss Marple Syndrome all over again."

I moved the phone further away from my face. "I don't have Miss Marple Syndrome," I said.

"You sort of do," Ruth said. "There was a murder? Who did it? Should I get my baseball bat?"

Ruth had little respect for matchmakers, no respect for coffee drinkers, but ever since I helped her with a mystery involving her family, she seemed to believe in my abilities as an amateur sleuth.

"I don't know who did it. I don't know if it was done. I mean, I don't know if he was murdered. But he wasn't a loved man, and his last words were that he was killed."

Ruth and Lucy said, "Ohhhhh" in unison.

"But he ate a lot of chips," I added, quickly.

"I'm going to tell Harry to get us on the first flight out of here."

"Don't stop your honeymoon," I insisted. "You only just started your round the world cruise. You're not even one-eighth of the way around."

"I'm not missing this. I keep missing all the fun. It's been forever since I stared down a serial killer."

"This isn't a serial killer. It's a one-shot deal killer. And I don't know if there's a killer. He ate chips!"

"You can't fool me, Gladie," Lucy said. "Harry, call the Concorde. What do you mean there's no Concorde? What happened to the Concorde? The world's gone crazy. Who loses a Concorde?"

She clicked off.

Ruth sat at my table. "I think your client did it," she told me. "That cursed man. Larry Doughy. Whatever happened to him has made his thinking off kilter. He's been going from one crazy-ass debacle to the other. Did you hear about the snakes?"

"I heard."

"There. See? He's off his nut."

"I think he's still getting checked out by doctors. He was nowhere near the murder. I mean, the death. I don't know if there was a murder."

But come to think of it, I had another match who was right there when it happened. The image of Cynthia knocking into Mike on her way out the door flashed through my mind. She had looked at Mike and had gotten upset. Why? Had he said something to her? Something so horrible that she killed him in some mysterious way?

Where was Cynthia now? I had to find her before Detective Nosy Hot Pants found her.

The door opened, and Spencer and his four remaining conference participants walked in. Spencer's face dropped when he saw me. He said something to Joyce and walked over to me.

"You stay out of it. Okay, Pinky?" he said without preamble.

"Good luck with that, copper," Ruth said. "She's already got the bug. Look at her."

He looked at me.

"Damn it, Pinky. Stay out of it."

I didn't like that he was saying more or less the same thing as Detective Super Hot. It made me feel like they were their own snooty country club, and I was an outsider who wasn't allowed to swim in the pool.

"I don't want anything to do with it," I said, raising my voice. "I'm a very busy professional. I have clients. I have a business. What do I care that you can't keep a guy alive in your police station, right under your nose? What do I care if a man gets murdered while you watched? Huh? Huh?"

"How did you know he was murdered?" he whispered.

"Wow. Gladie strikes again," Ruth said, impressed.

"Was he murdered?" I asked.

Spencer ran his fingers through his thick hair. "I didn't say he was murdered. Stay out it. You hear me, Pinky? I've got law enforcement from all over Southern California giving me their two cents and breathing down my neck. This has to be done by the book. All the I's dotted; all the T's crossed. Ruth, bring us a bunch of tea and whatever frilly crap you feed people to go along with it."

He stomped back to the table where the top cops were sitting.

"Frilly crap, huh?" Ruth said under her breath. "Don't worry, Gladie. I'll spy for you. Nobody notices the tea lady. You wouldn't believe the stuff I've heard in this place."

"You're going to help me?" I asked, surprised.

She shrugged. "Maybe I'm having a stroke."

While Ruth was spying for me, I drove to Cynthia's house. Lucy and Ruth were right about me and dead people. I found them everywhere, and I had a weird compulsion to figure out who murdered them. It was a disease. The Miss Marple Syndrome. But above and beyond that, Cynthia was my client. My match. I had gotten protective over my matchmaking. I had seen the power of happy endings, and I didn't want to deprive Cynthia of hers.

I parked in front of her house, but her car wasn't there. Normally, she parked in the driveway, because her garage was filled with her collection of antique cleaning tools. My phone rang.

"The cock crowed at midnight," Ruth said. "Come on. Laugh. You were supposed to laugh."

"I don't know what you're talking about."

"I know you're uneducated and ignorant, but I thought you'd at least have watched TV."

"My TV shows don't talk about cocks that do unnatural acts," I said.

"Do you want the rundown or not?"

"Give it to me."

"The top cop was murdered."

"Are we recapping? I thought we already knew that."

"I'm telling a story, Gladie," she explained. "A story starts at the beginning."

"Fine. The top cop was murdered."

"Guess how he was murdered."

"Ruth…"

"Guess."

"He was poisoned," I said. It was the obvious guess. He hadn't been shot, stabbed, or beaten to death. There was no poison gas and no aliens to laser him to death. No lightning and no electrical shock. It had to be poison.

"Duh," Ruth said. "What kind of poison?"

"I flunked chemistry, Ruth. I don't know poisons. Was it week old pot stickers from China House Buffet?" I loved that place. My grandmother was such a regular customer that they gave her free spareribs with every meal. Yum.

"You give up?" she asked.

"Ruth, you sound giddy. You're never giddy. Once you threw a guy out of your shop because he had too much positive energy."

"That guy made my teeth hurt. Nobody's that happy. The Dalai Lama's not that happy. Snow White's not that happy. Sick son of a bitch with his white teeth. He was lucky I didn't kick him in his white teeth. It used to be that folks had normal looking teeth. Now, everyone's got teeth so white they glow in the dark. White strips, my ass. Where's the priorities with these people? Used to be people cared about real things like social justice and labor rights. Not how white your teeth are."

"Okay, fine. Tell me what the poison was," I said.

"Daffodils."

"Excuse me?"

"You heard me, Gladie. Daffodils."

"The flower?" I asked. "The flower that's planted all over Cannes? The flower that the Daffodil Committee is fighting over?"

"That's the one," Ruth said. "Which means that the whole town is a suspect."

I looked at Cynthia's house. There was a wide swath of daffodils planted on either side of her front door.

Uh oh.

"Anything else?" I asked Ruth.

"Spencer made me pour two fingers of brandy into his tea. The top cops want to get in on the investigation, and he has to cart them around town while they do it. He's not a happy camper."

Spencer didn't like others honing in on his investigations. Now he had four egomaniac cops butting in. I wondered if that meant that Detective Nasty Waif Waist was off the case or not.

"Okay," I said. "Anything else?"

"Yeah. Larry Doughy's out of the nut farm, and he's looking for you."

After peeking into Cynthia's windows to search for her, I gave up on waiting for her and drove back to the police station.

While Spencer and the others were doing whatever they were doing, I was going to do some breaking and entering and a little stealing and a whole shitload of *na na na* for Detective Beotch Gorgeous.

I parked three blocks down the street from the police station. Luckily, I had my grandmother's dry cleaning in my trunk, which would be a perfect disguise. That's how I walked into the station dressed in a knockoff polka-dotted Givenchy dress with a wide, lime green belt, a faux fur bolero jacket, and a polyester scarf tied around my head. The sunglasses were mine.

I walked past the front of the station and peeked through the window, which was cut into the front door. There was no sign of Detective Bichitude Babe. Slowly, I opened the door. Fred was at the front desk.

"May I help you, ma'am?"

I didn't want him to have to lie to his superiors, not least because he was a terrible liar.

"I'm here to clean the upstairs toilets," I said in my best old lady voice. I walked quickly by him and down the hallway. I kept a lookout for unfriendlies, but I didn't have a lot of time. Sooner or later, Fred would remember that there wasn't an upstairs.

I found what I was looking for in Remington's office. The door had two names on it now. Remington's and Terri Williams. I tried the door handle, but it was locked. But I had lock picks in my purse, and I was particularly talented at using them. It only took a few seconds to break in.

The Mike Chantage file was right on her desk, where I expected to find it. I opened the file and took photos of every page with my cellphone without taking the time to read. I put the phone back in my purse and closed the file, leaving it the way I found it. I heard footsteps on the floor outside in the hall, and my skin prickled with fear. I had to get out of there in a hurry, but before I left, the framed photos on her desk caught my attention. They were the usual. One of her graduation with her parents. One on vacation on a beach in her bikini and her perfect body.

And there was one last photo of her in uniform next to Mike Chantage, the man who had been murdered a few hours before.

CHAPTER 6

Some matches are weird, dolly. Big, fat weirdos. But we're progressive, forward-thinking matchmakers. We don't discriminate on the basis of weirdo. In fact, I've matched a whole pile of weirdos. Remember when matching a weirdo, don't think you need to match him or her with another weirdo. Sometimes, a weirdo will love a non-weirdo and vice versa. But really, there's no rhyme or reason with weirdos. It's meshuga.

Lesson 50, Matchmaking advice from your
Grandma Zelda

I wanted to arrest Detective Guilty Gorgeous immediately. I wanted to point at her and yell, "she did it!" more than I wanted the Oreo company to make quadruple-stuffed Oreos, and I wanted that real bad. But I didn't have any proof that she killed Mike, whereas she hated me and had a gun, and I was reasonably certain she wasn't shy about using it. Somehow, I was going to have to gather all of my sleuthing skills in order to get her put away.

First thing was first. I had to get out of the building without her seeing me and poisoning me, too. I tied my grandmother's scarf tighter around my head and locked the office door behind me. I was anxious to get out fast in order to read the file, but I was careful to avoid as many people as possible. I walked close to the walls and peeked around corners. When I couldn't avoid a person, I lowered my face and hoped for the best. It worked. Nobody recognized me, and I got out with my stolen file images on my phone in my purse.

Boy, Spencer had crappy security.

Back in my car, after I removed my grandmother's clothes, I studied the images of the file. Detective Pretty Bitch had interviewed everyone, except for Cynthia. She had spent a lot of time grilling Arthur Fox and the waiter, who were the obvious number one suspects for poisoning Mike's food. But that was the problem, according to lab tests. There was no poison in his food or anyone's food. Mike Chantage had been poisoned earlier than lunch.

Poisoned with daffodils.

The interviews were all more or less the same. How had they known Mike? They had worked with him. Had he been acting differently? No. Had they seen anything out of the ordinary? No. Did they know of anyone who wanted to kill him? He wasn't a likable guy, but they didn't know anyone who would poison him. What are your thoughts on daffodils? They didn't understand the question.

I tapped my finger against my chin. There were a lot more questions I wanted to ask, but I would have to be careful. Spencer and Detective Moody Boobs wouldn't take kindly to me butting my nose in, and I didn't know how to interview the conference participants without Spencer finding out. Hmmm…I would have to think about that.

There was a knock on my car window, and I jumped, banging my head against the back of my seat. I peered out. "Larry? Is that you?"

Larry Doughy looked like hell. Half of his head was now bald, and his clothes were filthy. His eyes were wild. Crazy eyes. Obviously, he had only gotten worse since yesterday's snake incident. I was riddled with guilt, feeling that I should have protected him, somehow. Instead, I had been avoiding him and not taking his curse seriously.

I opened the car window. "Are you okay?"

"You gotta get this curse off of me. I don't know how much more I can take."

"The goat lady says she can do you tomorrow."

"What if I'm dead tomorrow? Or worse?"

From the looks of him, worse was definitely possible. "I'll

protect you," I said and instantly regretted my words.

"Do you have Mace? I think I need Mace."

"I have a travel-sized hairspray in my purse, and I know Krav Maga," I lied. His eyes stopped dancing, and he seemed to calm down a bit with the news of my weaponry.

"We should probably take your car," he said. "I've been using Uber, but the last guy caught fire."

I looked at my beautiful new car. It was older than spit but in pristine condition, and I had just gotten it. I didn't want it to be attacked by snakes or worse. But my guilt was overriding all of my other impulses, like survival. Larry Doughy was my client, my match, and he had already given me a deposit. Professional pride and moral decency were preventing me from fleeing for my life.

"Hop in," I told him.

Larry sat in the seat next to me and belted himself in. "Have you serviced this car recently? Have you checked the air in the tires?"

I had never done anything to the car except put gas in it. "Of course," I said. "Here we go."

"Where are we going? Someplace with no pointy corners?"

I didn't know how to answer that. "I have a few errands to run." I didn't have the heart to tell him that I was looking for a murderer.

I drove back to Cynthia's house after trying to get her by phone. She had disappeared, and I didn't know why, but I had a sneaking suspicion that she might have been involved in Mike's murder, even if I wanted Detective Gnarly Nipples to be the guilty one. If Cynthia really was the killer, Spencer would have my hide for bringing a murderer in to his station to kill one of his conference participants.

There was also the detail of Cynthia being my client. My matchmaking business had just begun to get off the ground, and I didn't want to derail it with a failed match, due to her being a killer.

Next to me in the car, Larry yawned. The poor guy probably hadn't slept since he had gotten cursed. After parking in Cynthia's driveway, I hopped out and checked all around her house for any sign of her. Nope. Nothing. I peeked in the windows, but there was no movement. I wrote a quick note and put it on her door. Then, I went back to the car. Inside, Larry was fast asleep. I closed the car door, quietly and sat for a moment, trying to decide what to do next.

A black van screeched to a halt a couple houses away, and two old ladies climbed out, one of them pushing a walker. They were dressed head to toe in black with black marks under their eyes, as if they were professional football quarterbacks. They looked around as if they were seeing if the coast was clear and then pulled out two large garden shears from the van. One old lady held the walker lady's shears while they walked, but they didn't have to go far. They hacked the hell out of the yellow daffodils with a terrifying ferocity.

Whack! Whack! Whack!

They went up the driveway, one on the right side and one on the left side, whacking the daffodils to their deaths until their little flower corpses littered the ground. Once they were finished with the driveway, they hit the daffodil beds in front of the house. When they were done, the one with the walker lifted her garden shears in the air and cackled a triumphant laugh. They looked around again, I assumed to see if the cops were coming, and when the coast was clear, they shuffled back to the van and took off with a screech of their tires.

Daffodil terrorists.

Ruth's words came back to me. "The whole town is a suspect."

I needed to talk to Morris, the head of the Daffodil Committee. He could give me insider information on psychotic Daffodil Committee members, although it did occur to me that Morris might have been the biggest psychotic Daffodil Committee member of them all. I called my grandmother. "Morris is at Bar None," she said, answering the phone. "There was a flower dust up, there. The bar had ordered white daffodil centerpieces for the Daffodil Competition, and the yellow daffodil contingent got angry. Pee before you get there, dolly."

She hung up. Larry was snoring next to me, his head

slumped against the window. I backed out of the driveway and made my way to Bar None.

The bar was hopping with customers, with nearly every parking spot taken. I recognized the daffodil terrorists' black van, and there were a couple of white ones next to it. "Where are we?" Larry asked, waking.

"Bar None. I have to talk to someone here."

"They deep-fry food here." He shuddered. "Being deep-fried's gotta hurt."

"It's a risk, I know, but they make the best chili cheese fries I've ever had."

The idea of chili cheese fries won Larry over. He also seemed calmer around me, like I was his talisman, even though we had been snaked together. Inside, the bar was dark, lit only by candles on the tables. Despite the darkness, Larry's entrance made a stir, and half of the patrons shifted in their seats, as if to make as much space between them and the cursed man.

"This looks pretty safe," he said, giving me his first smile since I had met him. My stomach growled. I was looking forward to the fries.

I looked around for Morris, but I heard him before I saw him. "White? White? Really?" he said to the manager. "The Daffodil Committee has patronized Bar None for sixteen years. Where's the loyalty? Where?"

"The Daffodil Committee ordered the centerpieces. Not me, Morris."

Morris choked and sputtered. "They… wha… huh… they… no!"

It was a cruel blow to Morris. He had traitors in his beloved Daffodil Committee. Those who wanted white daffodils instead of yellow. He turned around, searching the bar, probably for those who betrayed him.

"Morris," I said, approaching him. "It's me, Gladie. I was wondering if I could speak to you for a moment."

"What the hell are you doing here?" Spencer interrupted us, and he was giving me his "Lucy, you have some splaynin to do" look. He stepped between me and Morris, his large body blocking my line of sight.

"I…uh…huh?" I answered.

"I told you not to get involved."

I was disoriented. I couldn't figure out how he knew that I was getting involved. Did he have a third eye like my grandmother?

"I'm not getting involved," I lied. "I'm here with my match. You remember Larry."

Spencer flinched when he noticed Larry. Poor Larry. Even Spencer thought he was cursed. "And I was talking to Morris about…" I shut my mouth tight. Shoot. I had gone one step too far. If I mentioned anything about daffodils, Spencer would know exactly what I was doing. "Football," I said, finally.

Spencer leaned forward. "Football? Gladys Burger is talking about football?"

"Don't call me Gladys, and yes I'm talking about football. Nice talking to you, Morris," I said, even though I hadn't really spoken to him. "Come on, Larry, let's get some chili cheese fries."

"Spencer, you need to get CSI down here to take samples of all of the flowers in the back room of this place," Joyce Strauss ordered, stomping toward him before I could get to a table with Larry. She was at the bar, along with Sidney, Frank, and Leah. All of the conference participants were there. So, Spencer hadn't followed me. He didn't have a third eye. But they were ahead of me in the investigation. Way ahead. The only difference between us was that they didn't seem to know that Morris was the head of the Daffodil Committee.

"We're a town of two thousand people," Spencer told Joyce, annoyed. "We don't have CSI. But we'll get samples, Joyce."

Even in the dark bar, I could see him roll his eyes. Joyce was a pain in the ass, which was good for me because it took his attention off of my nosiness.

"Those flowers are going back," Morris said. "We don't want white daffodils here."

"What do you know about the daffodils?" Spencer asked him and shot me an I-know-what-you're-doing-here look.

My goose was cooked. I had to cover my tracks, quickly. "Go Bears! Go Dodgers!" I cried. I didn't know anything about football, but in my experience, lying followed by running away was always an effective tactic. I pushed Larry toward a table.

"This is a nice place," he told me, sitting.

"Yeah. Yeah. Whatever." From our table, I tried to hear what Morris and Spencer were talking about. It was like I was racing against Spencer to find the killer first. He had a whole team on his side, and I was on my own. But I was a dog with a bone, and Spencer had a detective who was a suspect. At least, I thought she was a suspect.

While Larry and I waited for our chili cheese fries, I fantasized that Detective Jerkface Belly Shirt was the murderer and I was the one to put her in the slammer. Oh, that would be satisfying.

Our fries and sodas arrived, and we dug in. "This is good," Larry said. "And nothing's happened for a while now. Maybe the curse is gone."

I didn't believe in curses, but I knew better than to tempt fate by saying that it might be gone.

Frank Fellows, the bully-type top cop, sat down next to me without being invited. "Gladie, right?" he asked me.

"I'm Larry. Larry Doughy," Larry said, smiling.

"Nice to meet you, man," Frank said but focused only on

me. "Did you hear about the daffodils?"

I dropped the fry that was halfway to my mouth. "Yes," I said.

"Weird way to kill a man, right?"

I didn't know where he was going with this conversation. Normally, police wanted me to stay far away from cases, and they never talked to me about them. "Weird," I agreed.

"Sounds like a woman killed him. Women use poisons." He stared at me, like he was trying to mind meld with me, or at least send me a hidden signal about women, poisons, and who the murderer was.

"They do?"

"Look at that woman," he said, gesturing toward Joyce, who was still giving Spencer a hard time. "Don't you think it's suspicious that she's sticking her nose in when it's not her case?"

I didn't think it was suspicious at all. I did it every chance I got. I nodded. "Suspicious, yes. Very suspicious. Why do you think it's suspicious?"

"Joyce hated Mike. Everyone knows that."

"What are we talking about?" Larry asked.

"Football," I said. "Why did she hate him?" I asked Frank, urging him to continue.

"I don't know. Mike had something on her. Mike was a bastard, and enjoyed making people's lives miserable. I would have killed him myself, but I would have knifed him in his throat, not kill him with flowers. I don't go that way, if you know what I mean."

"This is football?" Larry asked.

"Did he make your life miserable, too?" I asked Frank.

His face hardened and he stood. "Don't mind yourself about me. Joyce is the one you should focus on."

"I'm a matchmaker," I said.

"That's not what I hear," he said and walked back to Spencer.

"I don't know what's going on," Larry said.

"Errands," I explained and forked some fries and brought them to my mouth. But I didn't know what was going on, either. What did Joyce have against Mike? Was she honing in on the investigation in order to move the suspicions off of her? Why would she kill him with daffodils? Or maybe Frank killed Mike and was trying to pin it on Joyce. If not, why on earth would he have told me anything? We barely knew each other.

I checked out Joyce as she tried to order Spencer around. She was skinny and annoying, but she was all business. I didn't see her doing anything to prevent herself from moving up in law enforcement. She was gonzo ambitious.

But Spencer had had enough of her and was talking to Morris. Joyce walked away, obviously frustrated. I watched as she went toward the bathrooms. "I gotta go to the bathroom, Larry," I said.

"I'll come with you. The Coke is going right through me."

I cornered Joyce in the little alcove where the bathroom doors were. I plastered a wide smile on my face. "Joyce, I just wanted to tell you how inspired I am from your leadership."

She smiled back at me. "Just doing my job, filling in when there's gaps in the command structure."

I nodded in appreciation. "I hear you have your fill of suspects because Mike was, well, you know." I hoped she knew because I had no idea.

"I'm not at liberty to discuss suspects with you. Why? What have you heard?"

It wasn't easy trying to get information from someone who was trying to get information from me at the same time. "Just that Mike was, you know, not liked because, you know." Sheesh. I was getting nowhere fast.

"Mike was a highly respected law official. I don't see any reason for killing him except if it were someone he had tried to put away. Since he put away his share of bad guys, there's no shortage of suspects, but who? We don't know, yet. Yet," she added for dramatic effect, sticking her finger in the air.

"I really gotta go," Larry said and squeezed his way through us to the men's room. I had forgotten that he was there. Joyce took that moment to push past me to go to the ladies' room, which opened up and Leah Wilder came out.

Leah was the nicest of all of the top cops, and she promoted new, gentler methods of law enforcement. As soon as Joyce went into the bathroom, Leah cornered me. "Don't believe a word she says," she whispered.

"What do you mean?"

"Everyone hated Mike. Everyone. There wasn't a soul who came in contact with him who didn't want him dead. Do you know what that bastard did to my nephew?" I shook my head, no. "He beat him half to death during a drug bust. The man was sadistic in addition to archaic. And you probably guessed about the thing between Mike and Frank's wife."

So, that was the reason Mike kept making rude comments about Frank's wife. That made two more suspects.

"What about Detective Terri Williams?" I asked Leah. "She wanted him dead, too, right?"

"I don't know about her. I just met her. But what I'm saying is that Joyce is full of shit. She's bullshitting you and everyone else involved. You understand?"

I nodded. Joyce came out of the bathroom, and Leah walked out of the alcove, back into the dining area, as if she had never said a word to me. Joyce threw me an annoyed look as she passed me. Then, Spencer came into the alcove. It was the busiest place in the restaurant.

"What are you up to, Pinky?"

"About five-foot-seven."

"Pinky."

"I'm going to pee."

"What were you talking to Leah about?"

"Fine," I said. "Did you know that Mike Chantage beat up Leah's nephew and slept with Frank's wife?"

"Yes," Spencer said, matter-of-factly.

"What? What did you say?"

"Yes, I knew, Pinky. I'm the chief of police. And I'm not a moron."

"Oh." Spencer had been two steps ahead of me since Mike was murdered. For the first time, I felt that he was right about me butting in. I wasn't helping the investigation at all. He was ahead of me at every turn.

"Help! My wee wee is caught on the urinal!"

"Did you hear that?" Spencer asked me.

"Help! Oh my God! It's caught! It's caught!"

It was Larry, screaming bloody murder from the men's room.

"I didn't hear anything," I said.

"Pinky, that's your match. He's calling for you."

"You're the cop, and it's obviously an emergency," I said. "And it's the men's room. So, you go in and see about Larry's wee wee. I don't need to see his wee wee."

"I can't get it loose!" Larry cried from the bathroom. "Why am I cursed? Why? Why? I'll never use Twitter again!"

Spencer locked eyes with me and arched an eyebrow. He wasn't going to move. He wasn't going to check Larry's wee wee. We were deadlocked.

"You're going to let your girlfriend see another man's wee wee?" I asked him.

"Normally, I would be upset about that, but in this case, I'm thinking I don't have to worry. Let me know if we have to call the paramedics."

Spencer pushed open the door to the men's room and signaled to me to enter while he stayed on the outside. I closed my eyes and walked in.

"I'm here, Larry. What's wrong?"

"I flushed the urinal, and oh my God!"

I wasn't an expert on urinals. I knew men stood at them, peed, and flushed. That was about it. Yes, I had cleaned my share of toilets in my life, but I was a women's room toilet person and never crossed over to the other side.

The reason was that the other side had pee on the toilet seats, no matter how many urinals there were. And here was my secret, my pet peeve, my straw that broke my back: I couldn't stand pee on a toilet seat. It grossed me out. It made me gag. In my life of tripping over dead bodies and trucks full of snakes falling on my head, pee on a toilet seat might not have seemed to be a big deal, but for some reason, it was. It really, really was.

Luckily, Spencer had amazing peeing control and hadn't dripped a drop on my toilet seat. He must have had an ironclad prostate. A weather-proofed bladder. A penis superpower.

Spencer was obviously in the minority where men were concerned. Walking into the Bar None's men's room was proof that men were pigs with no control over their wee wees. There was pee everywhere. Urine covered every surface.

The smell was unbearable. I gagged and covered my nose with my hand.

The urinals were a modern version, weird contraptions with a complex, ornate flusher. The contraption had contrapted Larry, and he was hunched over it.

"Are you sure you can't get free?" I asked, not wanting to look too closely.

"I knew chili cheese fries would be dangerous," he moaned. "I'm never going to be able to have children now. You'll never be able to match me."

"Now, now," I said because I had no idea what else to say. He was right. He would be a hard sale if his wee wee was permanently caught in a urinal or worse.

"Come on, lady," Larry yelled. "I'm not a genius, but even I know that this is a non-starter for women."

"Now, now," I said, again. Boy, matchmaking sucked. It was a lot harder than people thought.

Larry's head flopped around in despair. "I'm stuck forever! I'm stuck forever!"

Poor bastard. Nobody deserved to be cursed, and Larry was a nice guy. He deserved to have a free wee wee. In fact, if miraculously he got out of this situation intact, I would bet dollars to donuts that he would go commando from now on.

I couldn't let my match suffer any longer. I had to help him. "I'm coming in!" I announced. I opened my eyes wide and inspected the damage. "Holy hell!" I shouted. "How did you do this to yourself?"

"Is it bad?" Larry asked, his voice quivering. "It's not that bad, right? I mean, you've seen worse, right?"

It was horrible. It was a nightmare. I would need therapy for the rest of my life. It was like a Hanoi Hilton / Stephen King combo. The producers of the *Saw* movies would take a look at it and say it was too gruesome for them.

It was bad.

"It's not too bad," I said. "We'll get you out of this, pronto."

I had bad spatial skills and was the world's worst with puzzles, so I couldn't figure out how to get Larry free. I worried that I was going to have to go old school in order to get him out of his predicament.

I was going to have to get hands on, in order to get Larry free.

"Larry, don't take this personally," I said. I took a deep breath and thought of England. I leaned over him and got into position. Then, I cupped his balls with one hand and fiddled his wee wee with my other hand.

That's when Spencer walked in.

"Okay, Pinky. I was just joking. Just paying you back for getting in my business in front of the others. I'll handle this." He froze in place and his eyes were fixed on my hands, which were giving Larry full on third base action.

"Are you cupping that man's balls?" Spencer asked.

"This is totally your fault," I said. "You said you didn't care."

"I didn't care about you seeing his balls, not cupping his balls."

"Balls," Larry moaned in a happy moaning way and magically, his wee wee came loose and he fell backward into Spencer's waiting arms.

"Pinky, we never speak of this again," Spencer said, holding Larry in his arms. Larry's lower half was naked, his nude buttocks leaning against Spencer's pants front, and somehow, my hand was still cupping his balls. "Never. Do you hear me, Pinky? Never."

CHAPTER 7

Maybe you should just give up. Let it go. You have a full life, plenty of other things to do. Easier things. These are all thoughts you will have from time to time, dolly. It's not a shanda to have them. Not a shame. They're normal thoughts. Who wants difficult when easy is so much easier? We grow up watching Cinderella sing, and we think that love is easy. How could it not be easy? It feels good. It makes you sing. But love is a bitch, bubbeleh. It's harder than calculus or those acrobat shows in Vegas. As hard as love is, matchmaking love matches is harder. It's not for wimps. So, if you're a matchmaker, keep going. Never give up. Once you're on the scent, don't quit. Follow it to the end. The happy ending.

Lesson 35, Matchmaking advice from your
Grandma Zelda

Larry was fine, but he would probably never pee in a urinal

again. After washing my hands for fifteen minutes and getting the rest of our chili cheese fries to go, Larry and I left. The trip to Bar None had been a total wash. I hadn't gotten any information on daffodils, and all I learned was that Mike was a sadistic adulterer and nobody liked him.

Fingers were pointing at Joyce Strauss, the skinny know-it-all who was defending Mike as a stand-up guy for some reason. But there was still the missing Cynthia, and I was hoping that Detective Stunning Nasty Ass was the real culprit.

Spencer packed up his top cops in his white van, but he waited to make sure that Larry and I were clear of Bar None before he drove off.

"Where are we going?" Larry asked, smiling at me. He had been doing a lot of smiling at me since the urinal incident.

"We need to regroup," I said. "Get back to home base and work on strategy."

My mojo was majorly screwed up. I was two steps behind Spencer in the investigation, I had lost one match, and I had cupped my other match's balls. I needed some sanctuary time.

I drove home and parked in the driveway. Grandma opened the front door before we got to it. "I've got fried chicken and mashed potatoes ready on the table," she told me. "Welcome, Larry. I put safety plugs in all of the outlets."

"Thank you, ma'am," he said.

I put the box of fries on the table, and Grandma and I dug in. Larry didn't eat because the chicken had bones, and that put the fear of God in him.

"I think my mojo is gone, Grandma," I said. "I'm getting nowhere. Spencer hasn't even called me Miss Marple. He's got a team of top cops, and they're leaps and bounds ahead of me."

"Are they?"

"Yes. Aren't they?" Grandma had a way of knowing things that couldn't be known, but she was crap at murder.

"I'm getting something," she said, like she was listening for alien contact over the radio. "I think you should get back to your matchmaking and everything else will fall into place."

"Nice try," I said.

"Love is everything," she said. And that was that. Love was everything to Grandma. I didn't think love would help in a murder investigation, but she would never accept that belief, so I kept it to myself.

Since I was at a standstill in my busybody activities, I decided to call it a day. Besides, I didn't know where Cynthia was and tomorrow was goat lady day. It was wiser to keep Larry in one place where he couldn't get in too much trouble. Grandma put him in the sun room because it had the least amount of furniture and a battery-powered television that wasn't connected to the grid. The second his head hit the pillow on the day bed, he was fast asleep and snoring softly.

With Larry taken care of, I took a shower and slipped into my bed. I turned on the television. A *Miss Marple* episode was playing, as if it was trying to shame me. In the show, Miss Marple was solving a complex murder while knitting a cardigan. There was no ball cupping for Miss Marple. No snakes. No being outwitted by the local cops. In fact, *she* was the outwitter. Always.

I flipped the channel to a *Saved by the Bell* rerun, which was more on my intellectual level these days. Spencer came into the room during the second rerun. Without saying a word, he took off his jacket, draped it over a chair, and loosened his tie. He stripped down to his birthday suit and got into bed next me, slipping his arm under my neck and pulling me in close to his side.

"You know what I've been thinking about for the past two hours?" he asked but didn't wait for an answer. "I've been wondering how I could get off if I murdered four top cops. I don't know why whoever killed Mike didn't kill the rest of them. Not a worthwhile lump of flesh in the bunch."

"Leah's kind of nice," I said.

"Sanctimonious sack of shit," he corrected. "Everybody's fighting with everyone else, so now they've broken up and gone their own ways. The conference is over, and I have four egomaniac cops in my jurisdiction for thirty-six more hours running wild like animals, all with their own theories about Mike's murder."

"Any theories you want to share with me?" I asked.

"Funny one, Pinky. You're off the case, and so am I. Terri's in charge of this investigation, and I'll let the four musketeers play around and leave none the wiser in a couple days. Okay?"

I didn't answer. It dawned on me that taking on the four musketeers would be easier now that they had split up and gone their own ways. That would be number two on my list for tomorrow. First up would be finding Cynthia.

"What are we watching?" Spencer asked, taking the remote control from me. "Family Guy's on now, you know."

Larry had gotten through the night and breakfast without mishap. We waited for Spencer to leave for work before we snuck out to find Cynthia. This time, we found her at home, and she wasn't alone. Sidney Martin was with her, and they were both glowing. Somehow, they had found each other again, and obviously sealed the deal.

"Gladie, you're the best matchmaker on the planet," Cynthia gushed when she greeted me. She let Larry and me in, and we all sat together in the kitchen nook, where she served us coffee and cherry Danish. She put her hand on Sidney's, and they gazed into each other's eyes. "We're getting married," she said.

"Next week, and then we're going on a cruise," Sidney added. "I'm retiring. I already sent my letter to headquarters."

"Cruises are fine if you're not cursed," Larry said.

"Huh?" Sidney asked.

It was quick. Very quick. They met and within twenty-four hours decided to get married, and Sidney decided to retire. The timing sent all of my red flags waving.

I took a bite of my cherry Danish, as if I wasn't at all surprised about the wedding. "This is great news. I'm so happy for you, Cynthia." I chowed down on the Danish while I tried to figure out how to segue into the murder and why Cynthia ran out of the conference. No matter how hard I thought, I couldn't figure out a natural transition from weddings and retirement to a discussion on motives and poison.

There was a loud knock on the front door, shaking me out of my thoughts. The knocking evolved into pounding. "What the devil?" Cynthia asked. She went to the front door and opened it.

"Cynthia Andre, you can't hide from me."

I knew the voice. It was the cold-hearted Detective Legs and Boobs. Drat.

"What do you mean?" I heard Cynthia say. "This is my house. I'm not hiding."

"You better talk to me. You understand?"

"I guess so?" Cynthia said like a question.

I heard the door close, and then they walked into the kitchen. Detective Hotsy Totsy's expression was priceless when she saw me. Gobsmacked. Thunderstruck. Flabbergasted.

"What are you doing here?" she demanded. I took another bite of the Danish, and Cynthia answered for me.

"Gladie was here to wish us well. She fixed us up."

Detective Fancy Pants looked from Cynthia to Sidney and back again. I could almost hear the cogs in her brain move, as she tried to take it all in. Her suspect and a witness—who could also be a suspect. Who knew? – were together, happy as clams, the day after a man was murdered. She was practically drooling.

I washed down the rest of my Danish with the coffee. One of the best parts of matchmaking was the food. "Ms. Burger, would you excuse us while I question Cynthia?" Detective Hot Bossy asked, but it didn't sound like a question.

"Sure," I said. "I'll clear the table with Sidney." I gave Sidney some elaborate signals with my eyes, and he caught on. We cleared the table, while Detective Hardass Hottie and Cynthia went into the living room to discuss the murder. I would have loved to be a fly on the wall, but at least this way, I had Sidney to myself.

"Quick," I whispered to him. "Tell me everything. Where was Cynthia? Why did she run out of the room? Why did you hate Mike?"

Sidney's mouth popped open. "I didn't hate Mike," he said. I put my hands on my hips and arched an eyebrow. "Okay. Okay. Of course, I hated Mike. Everyone did. He was a monster. He called Internal Affairs on me and said I was corrupt. It took me months to clear my name."

"That's bad," I said.

"No kidding. He was a bastard. But that's not the worst thing I heard about him."

Deflection. That's what it sounded like to me. He might have had motive but not as much as someone else.

"And Cynthia?" I asked.

"Her stomach was upset. That's why she ran out. She doesn't like chicken."

Didn't like chicken? How was that possible? I loved chicken. I wanted some chicken right that second. I would have eaten a chicken Danish. I didn't believe Sidney's excuse, and as a top cop, I couldn't believe that he believed it, unless he was lying to protect her. Cynthia's discomfort at the lunch was not about chicken aversion. It was something else. Something bigger. And there was the pesky fact of her bumping into Mike right before he died.

I wanted to grill Cynthia, but she was cornered in the living room, and I had promised to get Larry to his goat ritual.

"Will you tell Cynthia goodbye for me?" I asked Sidney.

"Sure thing, and she put this aside for you."

He handed me an envelope. A check for my services, I assumed. I put it in my purse and thanked him.

Larry and I got back in my car. "I don't get it," he said.

"You're a matchmaker, but you talk an awful lot about murder. Is that normal?"

"I'm a multi-tasker."

"I think that pretty detective did it. She's an angry person."

I slapped the steering wheel. "Yes! Thank you! That woman has an attitude. She could have definitely murdered him."

"I hope no one will murder me," Larry said, staring out the window. "I don't know how far this curse goes."

"We're heading over to the goat lady, now, Larry. Then, you can get on with your life, and I'm going to find you love, too. Don't forget that."

"That might be nice," he said, wistfully. "Those two seemed happy. I've never been on a cruise. I've always wanted to go to Puerto Vallarta."

I had never been on a cruise, either. Spencer and I were going on our first vacation together, and I was nervous about it. What if it changed things between us?

"I bet we can find someone to love you, who wants to go to Puerto Vallarta, too," I told Larry.

It turned out that the goat lady didn't just uncurse people. She also had a standing garage sale, three-hundred-and-sixty-two days of the year. She was closed for Christmas, Thanksgiving, and National Potato Day. The sale spilled out of her garage, onto her driveway and into the cul-de-sac where she lived.

Since I had had run-ins with animal rights activists in the past, I was nervous about the goat ritual. If it entailed hurting the goat in any way, I would have to stop it. Either way, I was anxious about the whole thing, so I had asked Bridget to meet us there. She said she knew where it was because she had bought her coffee grinder and pasta pot there.

Bridget's car was already parked by the house when we drove up. I spotted her combing through inventory on a folding table on the street.

"Here we go," I told Larry.

"I hope this works," he said.

"How could it not?"

It could not in a million ways. First off, it was an old lady with a goat. Second off, maybe Larry was just danger-prone like Ruth's grandniece, Julie. But I hoped the goat worked, not only because I didn't know how much more Larry could take, but also because I didn't know how much longer I could be Larry's escort in life. He was a nice guy, but I didn't look forward to him being my shadow for the rest of my life.

Bridget wasn't the only familiar face at Moses Rathbone's garage sale. Half of the uniformed police force was there, too. "Hello, Underwear Girl," Fred greeted me. He was holding a

Wonder Woman cookie jar, and he was considerably more relaxed than the last time I had seen him.

"Hello, there, Fred." I made the rounds, saying hello to everyone. "Are you all on your lunch break at the same time?"

"We're hiding from Detective Williams," Fred explained. "She scares me, and I need a break from butts."

"How much is this TV?" Officer James asked, pointing at a large screen on the lawn.

Everyone was loading up with used, discount goods. It was a free for all, and it was contagious. I found myself looking at knick-knacks, and suddenly I had the conviction that I couldn't live without a flashlight-can opener combo for seven dollars.

"Are you Moses? I'm Larry." Larry was introducing himself to the goat lady on the lawn, and I reluctantly pulled myself away from the tables. I grabbed Bridget on my way to join them.

The goat lady gave Larry a once-over. "That's a doozy creeper curse, Larry," she said, looking at him from the corner of her eye, while she took a wad of cash from one of the cops, who was buying enough stuff to fill a dorm room. He paid and put his shopping in the trunk of his police car.

"I'm running out of digits," Larry told the goat lady.

Moses nodded. "You didn't come too soon, that's for sure. The good news is that the goat is ready."

"The thing is," I interrupted. "Nothing bad will happen to the goat, right?"

"That depends," she said. "The last creeper curse put him off his feed for two days. He would only eat popcorn and Milk Duds."

"That doesn't sound so bad," Bridget said. She was right. Milk Duds sounded good.

"Okay. Just checking," I said.

"So, it really works, right?" Larry asked. "I'm going to be uncursed?"

"Yep," the goat lady said. "The goat chews your clothes and poops out the curse. Presto chango."

"That doesn't sound very scientific," Bridget told me.

I shushed her. "It's very scientific," I assured Larry. "Jonas Salk was the first one to use the method."

"I don't know what she's talking about," the goat lady said. "My grandmother taught it to me."

"And then Jonas Salk cured polio, but really, he's mostly known for his goat uncursing technique," I continued. I was desperate. We were down to the wire. Larry was almost uncursed. Then, I could match him and focus on showing up Detective Lady Pissant and revealing who killed Mike Chantage. If Larry didn't believe a goat could chew up his clothes, poop it out, and leave him free of more mishaps, we were screwed and that would be a major wrench in my works. Luckily, Jonas Salk's name still carried some weight.

"I can't wait," Larry said. "I have plans once I'm free."

Bridget patted Larry's back. "I hope you're free, soon." She sniffed and wiped a tear from her face. "Hormones," she whispered to me.

Moses positioned Larry on the lawn next to the goat and took some money from Fred, who had finished shopping. His arms were bursting, and I took a few items to help him to his car. While we walked to the car, the goat started to chew on Larry's pants.

"I feel it working, already," Larry announced, excitedly.

"The lady police captain was looking for you," Fred told me, as he opened his trunk.

"Leah?"

"No. The skinny one. She wanted to tell you something. Something about roses?"

My skin prickled, and I gasped. "You mean daffodils?"

"Maybe. She was bossing me around, too, but at least I didn't have to look up a butt for her."

There was a police siren, and all of the policemen at the garage sale looked at their cars, but the siren wasn't coming from them. The noise got louder, as a car turned into the cul-de-sac.

Uh oh.

It was Spencer's squad car. He screeched to a stop by the table of Adam Sandler bobble heads. Spencer stepped out, and so did a middle-aged woman, who was madder than spit.

"That's my television!" she shouted, as Officer James carried it to his police car. "And that's my entire living room set! And that...that's my goat!"

All eyes turned to the goat, which was halfway up Larry's pants leg.

"It's working! It's working!" Larry shouted. "I'm almost free!"

Officer James approached Spencer with the television in his arms. "I paid for this fair and square, Chief."

"You bought stolen goods?" Spencer asked. His face was bright red, and I was worried about him having a stroke. "You're all here, buying stolen goods? My police force is buying stolen goods? Stolen? Stolen?" Spencer's voice rose in pitch and level with each question.

Everyone looked at the ground.

"Larry, you think you're cursed? Buddy, I'm the one who's cursed," Spencer yelled. "I've got a big curse! An entire police force worth of a curse."

"I can take care of that curse, if you forget about this whole thing," the goat lady offered.

The woman who had arrived with Spencer, marched up the lawn and grabbed the goat's collar, yanking it away from Larry's pants. "You're a sick woman," she spat at Moses. "Taking an innocent goat to do immoral things."

"Wait," Larry pleaded. "My creeper curse."

But his pleas landed on deaf ears. The woman took her goat away, and the police packed away the stolen belongings. It turned out that Moses's garage sale was made up entirely of stolen goods and was part of a burglary ring, which was run out of the next town over. So, the good news was that Spencer's police force did six arrests, but the bad news was that in addition to the fact that one of his conference participants was murdered, Spencer had a police force decorating their homes with stolen goods.

Things weren't going well for Spencer. He was overwhelmed with bad news. Disoriented. It was the perfect moment for me to get involved and butt in where I wasn't supposed to.

Meanwhile, poor Larry Doughy was standing on the lawn, looking like Robinson Crusoe in his torn clothing and distraught.

"Maybe it was enough to fix the curse," I told him, trying to make him feel better.

The goat lady cackled, as she was being handcuffed. "Not a chance," she said. "No creeper curse can be cured when a goat only eats one and a half pants legs."

"Maybe she's wrong," I whispered to Larry.

"Power to the people!" Bridget shouted. "Down with police brutality!"

"Are you kidding me?" Spencer said.

CHAPTER 8

Danger, Will Robinson! I loved that show. Robots. Aliens. So much fun. Wouldn't it be nice if real life were like that? Actually, it might not be good to actually be lost in space. Not a lot of fried chicken in outer space. At least, I assume there's not a lot of friend chicken in outer space. But anyway, dolly, what I mean is danger. I mean, danger is dangerous. I mean, danger, bubbeleh! Danger! You'll understand when your match loves a man who's wrong for her, and you have to tell her. You'll understand when another match wants a woman known as, "the bitch of the southwest," and you have to tell him no. Be very careful is what I'm trying to tell you. There's a crapload of meshuganas out there. My friend Doris is permanently bald because she wasn't careful. Emmes, my hand to God, I'm telling you the truth.

Lesson 116, Matchmaking advice from your
Grandma Zelda

"Maybe you're partially uncursed. Enough uncursed to keep your digits. Maybe you're just cursed enough now to get the middle seat on planes or never win the lottery. That kind of thing."

Larry sniffed. "You think so?"

After watching the arrests, I coaxed Larry back into my car with the promise of lunch at Saladz. Bridget was following us in her car. Larry had cried on and off since we left the goat lady's house. I had tried everything to cheer him up, including singing songs from the Disney classic *Dumbo*. Nothing worked except for lying.

Lying took the edge off.

"Yes," I assured him. "Before the goat chewed one and a half of your pants legs, you had the creeper curse aura. Now it's only about one-quarter—I mean, one-tenth—of the creeper aura. You're practically aura free. Creeper curse aura free, I mean."

Larry wiped his nose on his sleeve. "My aura does feel a little lighter. Maybe the goat really helped."

"Saladz has a killer turkey and cranberry sauce sandwich that I'm sure will lift your spirits. And fries. Unless you prefer potato chips."

Killer turkey and cranberry sandwich. Killer. The word reminded me that I was getting nowhere closer to finding Mike's killer. Usually at this point, I was following a trail, and I had major inklings. But, I had no inklings. I was inkling-less. Everyone wanted to kill Mike. Now that I knew more about him, I was wondering if maybe I had killed him.

He wasn't a nice guy.

Still, the suspects weren't shy to divulge their motives to me. All except for Joyce Strauss and Cynthia and Detective Booty Bitch. They were closed-lipped, but even without them, there was no shortage of suspects. Sidney had been wrongly accused, Leah's nephew had been beaten, and Frank's wife had been laid. All reasons to lace Mike's food with daffodils.

Food.

Food.

Hmm…

The food at lunch hadn't been poisoned, so the caterer Arthur Fox was out as a suspect, but maybe he was back in as a suspect if he fed Mike something before then. Had he served a snack? Maybe coffee cake or gourmet cookies? Or breakfast? Was there breakfast? Did Arthur hate Mike, too?

Was I kidding? Anyone who spoke to Mike hated him.

Saladz was hopping for lunch. The three of us found a table in the center of the restaurant, surrounded by diners.

"What happened to your pants?" Jean, the real estate lady, asked Larry as she approached our table. She was wearing a hot pink power suit and was carrying a large briefcase.

"I was partially uncursed," he told her.

Jean arched an eyebrow at me. "I didn't curse him," I said.

"It wasn't my fault."

She didn't look convinced. "Whatever," Jean said. "I came over here to tell you that the house across the street has almost reached a resolution. The government finally gave the okay for the plane to be hoisted out of the house. You know what that means?"

It meant that the tourist season across the street would be over. I didn't know what else it meant. "Of course, I know what it means," I said.

"So does your honeybunch," Jean said. "He's been keeping tabs on the whole process. That means we have to have that talk again. You got to tell me if you're interested in moving into that house. Even though it's cursed."

Bridget and Larry stared at me, as if I had grown an extra head. Jean waved at a man at a corner table. "Gotta go," she said. "I've got a big fish hooked on for a McMansion by the pear orchards. Let me know what you decide."

We watched her plaster a phony smile on her face and saunter to the corner table. Then, Larry and Bridget returned to ogling me. "I've got a hankering for the turkey and cranberry sauce sandwich," I said, studying the menu. "How about you guys?"

"Are you marrying Spencer?" Larry asked. "I think you make a very nice couple."

"Or the BLT with avocado looks good, too," I said, still studying the menu.

Bridget put her hand on my shoulder. "Gladie, are you and Spencer getting married?"

I put the menu down. "Uh," I said.

"Is that what the vacation is about? You're eloping?" she asked.

"No. That's just a vacation. And I don't know if I'm going to go. I'm sort of off airplanes."

"But you're getting married?" Larry asked.

Sweat broke out on my forehead, and I struggled to find an answer. "I'm not going to get married until gay people are allowed to be married," I said, finally.

"Gay people are allowed to be married," Bridget said. "Don't you remember my hunger strike?"

"Was that before or after the town hall sit in?"

"Before the sit in but after the Facebook protest and signature collection."

"Oh. So, gay people can get married, huh?" I asked.

"Yes."

"So, who can't get married?" I asked.

"I don't know."

"Come on. Someone must not be allowed to get married," I said. "There's got to be injustice out there, somewhere."

"Married people can't get married," Larry announced with glee. "You know, because they're already married."

I pointed at Larry. "There! There! I'm not going to get married until married people can get married."

Bridget sighed. "I'm sensing some adjustment problems, Gladie."

"Tell me about it."

"I don't blame you, though," Bridget said. "Marriage is no more than a father's need to sell off his daughter so she's not an economic burden."

"Really?" Larry asked. "That makes me look at marriage a whole new way. Marriage is really an archaic, misogynistic ritual, which imprisons a woman to a life of servitude and breeding against her will."

At the tirade against marriage, Bridget's eyes grew bright, and she smiled wide. "I'm Bridget," she gushed and flipped her hair. She pushed her glasses up the bridge of her nose and gave Larry her best come hither stare. Uh oh. I had to save Bridget from getting involved with Larry, even if he was only one-tenth cursed. After all, she was bringing a new life into the world.

I put the menu in front of my face and leaned over to Bridget. "He's a log cabin Republican," I whispered, and her face dropped in disappointment. Outside of a hippie commune in Humboldt, there weren't a lot of men who shared Bridget's worldview. Now she was preparing to be a single mother, and I imagined she would have liked to have a partner in her life for this momentous event, even if marriage was an archaic, misogynistic ritual.

I shuddered. As a matchmaker, I didn't have anything against marriage. It was just thinking about *my* possible marriage that gave me hives.

"I think I'll have dessert before the sandwich," I said. Larry and Bridget thought that was a brilliant idea, and we all started our meal with pie a la mode.

After we finished our lunch, Bridget had to get back to tax season, so we parted ways. I hugged her goodbye.

"By the way, I got a weird text from Lucy," she told me, as we stood on the sidewalk. "Something about a plane, a boat, and murder."

"She mentioned to me that she might be coming home early," I said.

"I hope nothing's wrong."

"I don't think so," I said. "She doesn't want to miss anything with the murder, but this is the most boring murder I've ever come across. Everyone's a suspect. Poison is boring, and nobody cares that the murder victim is dead." I shrugged. "I really should start matching Larry instead of dealing with this investigation."

"It's sounds like a dud of a murder. Like stale cereal."

"Exactly," I agreed. "Just like two-week old Corn Flakes."

Larry and I drove away in my car. "That was a nice lunch," he told me. "Relaxing. And I didn't burn myself or even bite my tongue. I even went to the bathroom without incident. That goat's amazing."

I sighed in relief. Finally, Larry was coming around to himself again. He felt so much better that he decided it was all right for me to take him home. He lived up further in the mountains, and it was a beautiful spring day. We opened our windows and enjoyed the fresh breeze and the scent of wildflowers, as we drove on the highway just outside of town.

"I have a feeling, Larry, that you're going to be totally fine. No more curse. No more bad luck. Just smooth sailing for a while. You'll be able to live your life, go to work, and find a special someone."

"That sounds really good. I could use my Jacuzzi again without fear."

"I'm glad we got you to the goat before it was confiscated."

"It was a light dose, but it seems to have done the trick," he agreed. "How long do you think it'll take you to find me my true love? I wasn't looking before, but all this talk about love and marriage has given me a hankering."

"I don't think it'll take that long," I said, and I was telling the truth. Without the curse, Larry looked good on paper and not so bad in real life, once his hair grew back in. There were scads of single women in town who would have been happy to date him.

"Are you going to keep looking into the murder? That sounds scary," he said.

"I'm not scared. I've done this before, and it's not a big deal. I have a lot of suspects with this one, though, but my money is on Joyce Strauss." I wanted it to be Detective Snobby Sexpot, but Joyce Strauss was a safer bet. She was the only one who said nice things about Mike, and that was a tell. She was the one.

"Is that the policewoman who looks like a model?" Larry asked.

"No, Joyce is a skinny school marm policewoman with pursed lips and an annoying know-it-all attitude."

There was a sound behind me, and Joyce Strauss's face appeared in my rearview mirror. It took me a moment to understand what was happening. At first I thought I had conjured her in my mirror, because I had been talking about her. But after a second, I realized that she had been hiding in the back seat on the roomy floor of my Oldsmobile Cutlass Supreme.

Joyce put a gun to my head with one hand and a knife at my throat with her other hand. I gasped, and the car swerved.

"Get the car under control," she yelled.

Somehow, even with the blood in my veins pumping a mile a minute, I managed to get control of my car and keep driving down the highway, like we were still on a pleasant ride in the spring weather.

"That's it," Joyce said in a threatening tone that made me shiver in fear. "Keep going straight. Follow the road."

"What's going on?" Larry demanded.

"Sit still and don't move a muscle, or I'll slice her open and blow a hole through her brain," Joyce told him.

Larry did as he was told and sat stiff as a board in his seat, but his eyes never left the scene between Joyce and me. I was an out of shape woman, and I wasn't a physical threat to anyone, but Joyce wasn't taking any chances. Not only was she going to kill me, she was going to stab me and shoot me at the same time. It was the definition of overkill.

"Hello, Joyce," I croaked. "How are you?"

"How am I? How am I? How can you ask that?"

"I'm a polite person."

Joyce sneered. I tried to drive carefully, but my eyes darted to the rearview mirror constantly, and the car swerved dangerously. Unlike other murderers that I had known, Joyce seemed completely sane. No crazy eyes. No twitching. She looked like a perfectly normal, middle-aged woman, who just happened to be holding a gun and a knife to my head. That fact scared me more than anything. She was clear-eyed and clear-headed. Determined.

"Joyce, what's going on?" I asked.

"You're going on. You! You've been sticking your nose in where it doesn't belong. Butting in."

It was a common complaint where I was concerned. I was a buttinksi. But this was a notch above the regular reaction to my busybodyness.

"I'm sorry. As a matchmaker, I get involved in people's lives. I guess it's a habit, but I'll stop. I promise. I used to have a nasty habit of cracking my knuckles, but I stopped that cold turkey. I'm sure I could stop this, too."

"Too late," she said, pushing the gun against my temple. "You've been asking too many questions, stirring things up."

"I have?" I had been asking questions, but I didn't think I had stirred up anything at all.

"You know you have. Mike was murdered. Let law enforcement handle it. They'll find the killer. That's all that counts."

I was confused. "You want them to catch you?"

"Me? What are you talking about? I'm not the killer."

"Oh. My mistake."

"If you're not the killer, why are you doing this?" Larry asked. It was a great question. Right on the nose.

"Because this one is butting in."

I sighed. We were on a loop with no hope for getting off it and no hope of getting out of this alive. Joyce was upset that I had "stirred things up" and asked a lot of questions, but not that I was searching for the murderer. If Joyce wasn't the killer, I couldn't figure out what she was upset about.

Unless.

"I asked questions, but I didn't find out about you," I told her, catching on. She was worried about shining the light on something about her.

"Baloney. You've been pestering everyone from the conference nonstop. I've heard about you, don't think I haven't. You've turned up more killers than Miss Marple. Nothing gets past you. You're the secret breaker."

"You're giving me a lot of credit that I don't deserve." But I was secretly tickled that I had that reputation. More killers than Miss Marple? Nothing got past me? The secret breaker? Those were all great things, and I wondered if they were true. Since moving to Cannes, I had stumbled on a lot of dead people, but I had never thought of myself as particularly gifted at solving mysteries. I was called the "murder magnet," but never the "mystery maven."

"That may be true," I told Joyce. "But not this time. This time, I've been two steps behind Spencer and you guys. I'm not any closer to figuring out Mike's murder. I don't even know how he was killed. I know it was daffodils, but I don't know how he ingested the flowers."

"Bullshit," Joyce said.

"She's telling the truth," Larry said. "She matched Cynthia and partially uncursed me, so she hasn't had time. She doesn't know who the murderer is."

It warmed my heart to see Larry protective over me. I hadn't done much for him in the way of uncursing him or finding him a match, but here he was, standing up for me in the face of an armed woman.

Then, out of the corner of my eye, I saw Larry fiddle with his seatbelt, and I was gripped with fear for him. It looked like he was planning to do something heroic, and I was worried that it would get him or me killed.

I had to cool the situation quickly before Larry made a move. With my sky-high blood pressure and pounding heart, my brain finally clicked into action.

"Nobody talked about you, Joyce," I told her, as calmly as possible. We were still driving on the highway up the mountains and approaching a long bridge, which spanned the distance between two mountains. "I didn't find out a thing about you. Nothing. I know that you're a very accomplished top cop and that's it. I promise."

I watched in the rearview mirror, as Joyce's face softened

ever so slightly.

"Bullshit," she said, but with less force and conviction than the last time she said it to me. It was my time to push forward and save us.

"I swear, Joyce. That's all I know. I found out that Mike slept with Frank's wife, that he beat up Leah's nephew during a drug bust, and he accused Sidney of wrongdoing. But you remain the secret. Top secret. A vault. Nothing. Please believe me. Nothing."

"Nothing?" she asked. She removed the knife from my throat, but she kept the gun at my temple.

"Nothing. Nothing at all. Zilch. Nada."

"Oh. I thought that…"

Then, it happened. Larry threw off his seatbelt and leaped across the seat, grabbing for the gun. My life flashed before my eyes, and it sort of fast-forwarded to Spencer, to an image of us lying in bed together, watching *Family Guy*, and right then and there, I knew I wanted to marry Spencer, if that meant being with him forever. And right then and there I knew I would do whatever it would take not to lose him, and right then and there, that meant not having my brains blown out.

Larry got hold of the gun, and he tussled with Joyce, their arms knocking into my head over and over. I tried to duck down, and the car swerved, drifting over the lanes, as we reached the bridge.

"You can't take a cop's gun," Joyce chastised Larry.

"I won't let you hurt her!"

"I wasn't going to hurt her!" Joyce yelled.

"Yeah, right!" Larry shouted back, struggling with her.

I had to give it to Joyce. For a skinny woman, she sure was strong. I, meanwhile, was having a dickens of a time, trying to maintain control of the car. I stomped my foot on the brake, but they hit me again as they fought for the gun, and I fell onto the steering wheel, making the car spin.

Car spinning and brakes screeching look different on TV than they do in real life. First off, on television, a stunt driver is driving. In real life, unfortunately, I was driving. And I didn't want to be driving. I didn't want to be in the car. Second off, unlike stunt drivers, I had no control over the car at all, and it was heading right for the bridge's guardrail.

There weren't a lot of ways I wanted to die. Even old age scared the bejeezus out of me. But driving off a bridge was way down the list, just below being eaten by a tiger and just above being burned alive.

"I got it!" Larry announced, ecstatic, finally holding the gun in his hand, away from Joyce. It was a great achievement on his part. Heroic. He held up the gun, thrilled with himself. Meanwhile, the car kept spinning, and the guardrail kept getting closer, and that's when poor, cursed Larry Doughy, who wasn't wearing a seatbelt, flew out of the open window that he had opened to enjoy the spring air.

I watched in horror as he went right through the window, his eyes huge as if he couldn't believe what was happening. The gun was still clutched in his hand, and out he went in the spring air, scented with wildflowers.

"Fuck you, Twitter!" he yelled and then he was gone.

The car finally came to a stop, but Larry didn't. He kept going up and over the guardrail and off the side of the bridge, as if he had wings.

CHAPTER 9

The end. Remember the time in Rocky where he was down, and you thought it was over for him, but then he got up and fought the other guy and won? That was good. But bubbeleh, not everyone is Rocky. Not everyone gets up after the end. Sometimes, the end is the end, and there's nothing we can do about it. So, this is a little smartness from me to you: sometimes love goes forever, but sometimes love has a beginning and an end, and when it's the end, it's the end. And just because it's the end, it doesn't mean that they can't live happily ever after.

Lesson 15, Matchmaking advice from your
Grandma Zelda

I turned off the car, jumped out, and ran to the guardrail. Joyce was right behind me. We leaned over the rail and looked down. I didn't want to look, didn't want to see Larry's body broken on the road beneath us that ran between the mountains.

"Where is he?" Joyce asked. "I can't see him."

Below us, way down below us, was an old road with few cars on it, but there was no sign of Larry.

"Help!" I heard him yell.

"Where are you?" I called back.

"Here!"

I leaned further over the side of the bridge, and then I saw Larry. He was right below me, bent over a highway sign, which announced that Cannes was five miles away. "Am I alive?" he asked, doubled over the sign and clutching its underside. He was too far away for me to reach him to help him up.

"I'm calling 911!" I announced.

I ran back to the car and called 911. It took some explaining, but they said they would be there in five minutes.

"Keep holding on!" I yelled when I returned to the place where Larry went over.

"Okay!" Larry called back.

"You did this to him," I said to Joyce, giving her a good push.

"I didn't mean any harm," she whined, all of her

aggressiveness gone.

"You didn't mean any harm with a knife and a gun? With breaking into my car?"

"Don't you understand?" she asked. "My career was on the line. I…"

Joyce didn't finish her sentence. Her eyes grew wide, and she coughed violently. She clutched her chest and gasped for air.

"What's the matter?" I asked. "Do you have allergies? What's going on?"

Her body heaved. "Make my killer pay," she croaked.

"What?"

Joyce's stomach roiled, and she doubled over, vomiting violently.

"This isn't good," I said. "This is bad. Real bad. Why is this happening? Don't do this, Joyce. Don't do this."

She fell onto the ground, and I dropped to my knees to help her. She rolled onto her back and looked up at me.

"I know," she whispered, her voice small and gravelly. "I know who killed me."

Joyce Strauss died in my arms on the pavement of the

highway that leads from Cannes up further into the mountains. She died without telling me who had killed her.

As she drew her last breath, a car drove across the bridge and stopped in front of us. A man stepped out and walked in our direction. It was Spencer. On second thought, it wasn't Spencer. He looked like Spencer, but he was slightly taller and bulkier, and he walked different.

"Spencer?" I asked.

He knelt in front of us and took Joyce's pulse.

"Are you all right, physically?" he asked me.

"I didn't kill her. She just died all of a sudden. I think it was poison. But I didn't poison her."

"I know you didn't kill her," he said. He had Spencer's eyes. Deep blue, rimmed with long, black eyelashes. He had Spencer's thick hair, too, but it was cut differently, and he was well-dressed like Spencer. Like a cross between a model and a hedge fund manager.

"You didn't answer me. Are you hurt...physically?"

"No, but my friend is hanging over a sign," I said, pointing.

The man who wasn't Spencer looked over the side of the bridge, and then he ran to his car and opened his trunk. Quickly, he threw off his shoes, his jacket, and his shirt. He grabbed rope from the trunk and ran back to the spot where Larry went over the side.

I could hear the sound of emergency services sirens in the distance, coming closer. Spencer's lookalike tied an intricate knot to the guardrail and went over the side without a moment to reconsider or wet his pants.

"I hope he doesn't die," I said to Joyce's body.

"I'm going to save you," I heard him say to Larry. "Don't fight me when I get to you. Otherwise, we'll both wind up two hundred feet down with every bone in our bodies broken. And contrary to belief, that would hurt like a bitch. So?"

"I won't fight you," Larry said. "But I may be cursed."

"Aren't we all, buddy. Aren't we all."

Two minutes later, they were back up on the bridge. Larry only had a broken toe, a miracle that he credited to the goat. Emergency services reached the bridge, while the hero who looked like Spencer was putting his clothes back on.

I recognized Spencer's car with the emergency services, which parked a couple feet away from me. The paramedics arrived first and checked out Joyce, allowing me to get up and walk to Spencer.

"Pinky, what did you do now?"

"It wasn't my fault, and I didn't kill her."

"Of course she didn't kill her," the man who had come to Larry's rescue said.

Spencer turned, ready with his meanest cop face, probably ready to tell the guy to back off and mind his own business, but the moment Spencer saw the good Samaritan, his face changed. His mouth opened in a large O, which then transformed into a wide, open-mouthed smile.

"Peter! Peter! Peter! Peter! Peter!" he yelled, like he was twelve years old at the midnight release night of the next Grand Theft Auto videogame. Then, Spencer did something I had never seen him do before. He jumped up and down.

"Peter!" he yelled again.

"Little brother!" Peter yelled back and pulled Spencer in for a bear hug.

Little brother. Ahhh… Of course. The guy who looked like Spencer was Spencer's older brother. That made a lot of sense.

After a long hug, Spencer slapped his brother on the back. "What're you doing here? I didn't know you were visiting."

"I missed my little brother," Peter said, smiling. "You're going to let me buy you dinner, right? You and your lady, of course." He winked at me, and my heart did a little flutter. I liked him immediately.

"How did you know I'd be on this bridge?" Spencer asked him.

"He saved Larry," I told Spencer.

Spencer put his arm around Peter's shoulders. "That's what my brother does. He saves people wherever he goes. That and other things, but if I tell you about the other things, I have to kill you. Am I right, bro?"

"Don't worry," Peter told me. "I'd kill you, but I'd make it look like natural causes. It wouldn't hurt at all."

Spencer guffawed, loudly, and I smiled out of politeness.

"Now Pinky, tell me how you killed Joyce," Spencer said.

The paramedics took Larry to the hospital to give him a complete once-over, while I spoke for forty-five minutes about Joyce and her trying to kill me before she threw up and died. Forty-five minutes didn't seem to be enough for Spencer, because he insisted that I go to the station to make an official statement.

Spencer's brother, Peter, went, too.

The station was a hive of activity because the remaining three conference participants had heard about Joyce's death, and they came, wanting answers. Spencer sat me in the lobby with a pad of paper and a pencil.

"Write that up, Pinky, while I handle the mess."

"I'll keep her company, and when you have time, let's talk

a minute before we go to dinner," Peter said, sitting in the chair next to me and crossing his legs.

Spencer smiled, obviously delighted. "He's going to keep you company, Pinky. Isn't he wonderful? What a guy! What a guy!"

I had never seen siblings get along this much. Spencer wasn't the buddy-buddy kind of guy, and it was a surprise to see him bosom buddies with anyone, let alone his big brother. I was an only child with a terrible relationship with my mother, so this kind of brotherly love was foreign to me.

Fred walked by with a man in handcuffs. "Hello, Underwear Girl," he said. "Detective Williams gave me another one to process. This one was busted for ecstasy."

"Hey, the ecstasy was for my dog, man," the convict insisted.

"Then, why did you put it up your butt?" Fred asked. "You think your dog wants butt ecstasy? I don't think so, pervert."

"Fred has been on butt detail for the past few days," I explained to Peter.

"My sympathies, Fred. But obviously the chief believes that you have both a sensitivity and a competency to do this difficult work. Hats off to you, my man. Hats off to you."

Fred stood taller and seemed to think about Peter's words. "I am sensitive," he said.

"The first moment I saw you, that's exactly what I thought," Peter said and winked at me.

I wrote up my statement, giving the details about the gun and knife and how Larry tried to save me and how Peter saved Larry. "Done," I told Peter when I finished.

He looked over my shoulder at my statement. "Would you mind if I make one small editorial change?"

"Uh, no?"

I handed him the paper and pencil, and he erased everything about him in my statement. "Is that legal?" I asked. "That's an official statement."

Peter shrugged. "In my experience, 'legal' is up for debate."

"But why don't you want anyone to know that you saved Larry?"

"I like to keep a low profile. Do you like steak? I'm feeling like a big steak and a bigger martini for dinner."

"I like steak," I said, but what I really wanted to say was, "who the hell are you?" He was like Spencer up to a point. Like Spencer, he was sexy as hell, a perfectly coiffed and dressed metrosexual, but whereas Spencer stopped at animalistic manly manliness, Peter continued with a cosmopolitan, worldly James Bond thing. He seemed perfectly happy at all times, relaxed, content, like no matter what happened, he would be totally fine.

Spencer came back into the lobby with Sidney, Frank, and Leah. "You can't force us to stay in town," Frank growled at Spencer.

"Listen, Frank, you're on my beat now. You get me? So, you'll stick around until I'm satisfied. Are we clear?"

Frank was big and smelly, but Spencer was big and smelled good. Frank was annoyed, but Spencer was fed up. "I'll give you forty-eight hours," Frank told Spencer.

"That's enough. We good here?" he asked the rest of them, and they nodded. When they left, Peter stood and smoothed out his suit. He gave me his hand and helped me up.

"Little brother, how about we all go into your office and talk a minute before we go to dinner?"

"Absolutely," Spencer said, giddy. "I'll show you my new Glock. You're going to love it."

Peter and I sat in the chairs facing Spencer's desk, and Spencer handed his brother his gun after he took out the bullets. "Pretty," Peter said, approvingly.

"Joyce Strauss tried to kill me," I said, breaking into the family reunion. "She put a knife to my throat and a gun to my head. She didn't like me butting in about the murder."

"Gladie likes to butt in," Spencer explained to Peter.

"I know. You've told me."

"You have?" I asked.

"Spencer used to only talk to me about baseball and interrogation techniques. Now it's all you, Gladie," Peter explained.

The two handsome men stared at me, and I felt my face turn bright red. I fanned myself with my hand and tried to catch my breath.

"Joyce tried to kill me," I repeated, trying to get back on track.

"I think she was trying to scare you," Spencer said.

"She did a good job."

"Something went down between her and Mike," Spencer continued. "I'm thinking he had something on her, and she didn't want it to come out. What do you think, Peter?"

"I think that's a safe bet, but I'm afraid I have to add something to the mix."

Spencer leaned forward. "No way."

"Way," Peter said, nodding.

"No way!"

"Way."

"No! Way!"

"Way."

"What are we talking about?" I asked. "What way?"

Peter turned to me. "I'm sorry, Gladie. It turns out that Mike Chantage was dirty dealing. International dirty dealing."

"What does that mean?" I asked.

"Mike was a spy," Peter and Spencer said in unison.

Once again, I was confused. I didn't know how Spencer's brother would know anything about Mike, let alone that he was a spy.

"Let me explain," Peter told me. "Actually, I can't explain, but let me give you hints."

"She loves hints," Spencer said.

"Now and then, I come in contact with people like Mike," Peter explained.

"A jerk? An adulterer? A blackmailer? A liar? A sadist? Or a spy?" I asked.

"All of the above, but I was referring to the last one."

Spy. Spencer's brother came in contact with spies. So, that meant that he was either a spy, himself, or he was a spy catcher.

"Isn't he awesome?" Spencer said, gushing over his brother.

SCAREPLANE

After dinner, Spencer and I returned home, and Peter went wherever spy catchers went to bed. My grandmother was already sleeping, and the house was dark and quiet. Spencer locked the front door, and we walked upstairs slowly. I was exhausted. It had been a hell of a day. I was physically, mentally, and emotionally worn out.

Once we were in my bedroom, we closed the door and started stripping down, throwing our clothes on the floor. I was planning on going to bed without brushing my teeth.

"I'm so excited that Mike was a traitor," Spencer whispered. "Now Peter will stick around for a day or two."

"That was good luck."

"It'll be a treat to watch Peter work, hunting down KGB or terrorists or whatever. Hey, Pinky," he said, putting his finger under my chin and tilting my head up. "I'm sorry that bitch scared you today."

"I almost died. Larry almost died. Joyce actually died."

Spencer nodded. His eyes were sad and searched mine for something. "You're not allowed to die, Pinky. You can't die because that'll kill me. You can't die because I have big plans where you're concerned. You can't die because I love you."

I tried to swallow, but there was something in my throat. Probably my heart. My eyes filled with tears and spilled over.

Spencer wiped my cheeks with his thumbs.

"She said I was a buttinski," I said.

Spencer shrugged. "Just because she was a psychotic bitch doesn't mean she wasn't smart and perceptive."

"Somebody poisoned her, and I don't think she was a spy."

"Again, she was perceptive and smart. Maybe she knew Mike was a spy and knew who killed him."

Spencer had a point. Joyce could have known too much and had to be daffodilled to death. The daffodil angle bothered me, though. It didn't sound like a sophisticated spy way to kill, as far as I was concerned.

Spencer kissed me lightly on my eyelids and down my cheek to my neck. He wrapped his arms around my waist and pulled me in close. He smelled so good. I couldn't get enough of smelling Spencer. I nuzzled his neck and put my hands on his stomach, between us.

"Have I told you recently that I love you?" he asked, working on giving me a hickey.

"You just told me."

"Oh. How about your ass? Have I told you recently that you have the hottest ass? Jennifer Lopez is a dog in the ass department compared to you."

I put a finger on his lips to shut him up. "Let me give you

a hint, here, Spencer. Don't talk about other women when you're trying to seduce me."

"Do not try. Do," he said in his best Yoda voice.

"And don't do your Yoda voice when you're trying to seduce me."

"You have a lot of rules. How about my tongue? Can I use that?"

"That's a good point," I said. "The tongue is good, but wagging it is bad."

He picked me up and wrapped my legs around him. "Maybe I should give up trying to seduce you, since I'm so bad at it."

"You know what they say: Practice makes perfect."

"Good point. Good point," he said, laying me gently on my bed. He separated my legs and leaned down.

"Now about my tongue," he started and then there were no more words.

Spencer was good at making love and good at loving. After we were finished pleasuring each other, he fluffed the pillows and held me in his arms, cuddling under the covers.

"It's kind of amazing that people keep dropping dead around you," he whispered.

"Normally, they're already dead when I find them."

Spencer yawned. "It feels great having Peter around. It's like I have a partner to fight crime with. Not like my idiot police force. I've got the only police force in history that was instrumental in keeping a burglary ring in business."

"I think they were using shopping as a break from your new detective."

"Terri? She's been great. A real hardass."

I wanted to tell Spencer to fire her, to tell him that Detective Fart Face Bangin' Bod was mean to me, and she had to go. But that broke every dating commandment in existence.

Anyway, I didn't need to worry about her anymore because I had decided to put Mike's murder far behind me. Ditto Joyce. The two of them were horrible people and maybe traitors to the country. From here on out, I was going to let Spencer's brother and whoever else wanted to, to investigate the murder and find the killer.

I was done. Finished. Retired from snooping. No more Miss Marple. No more knives and guns and bridges and daffodils.

The thought calmed me, and with my head on Spencer's chest, hearing the beat of his heart and his breathing, I fell into the deep sleep of the innocent.

CHAPTER 10

Organization is the key to success, dolly. I'm not the first to say it, and I won't be the last. I keep a lot of the business in my head, but don't be fooled by that. I'm organized, and you should be too. An ounce of organization is worth a pound of Tylenol. You get what I'm saying? Don't get a headache. Organize.

Lesson 82, Matchmaking advice from your
Grandma Zelda

"I'm the one with jet lag, but you're the one sleeping? How's that fair?"

I opened my eyes. Lucy was standing over me.

"You're in Thailand," I said.

"I was in Thailand. They've got big bugs there, darlin'. I almost put a saddle on one of them and rode it around. But you need me. I heard there was a second murder."

"You heard that in Thailand?"

"Harry has good sources."

I sat up in bed. Spencer had gone to work already. I checked the clock. Eight-thirty. I had overslept.

"Two murders, and I was there for both of them," I told her.

Lucy sat at the foot of my bed and crossed her legs. "I miss everything. Why are planes so slow? I could have at least caught the second murder."

"It was another daffodil murder," I explained. "She was flowered to death."

"Flowered to death," Lucy repeated, as if she was tasting the words on her tongue. "Don't that beat all. So, where do we begin?"

"I'm retired. I'm letting Spencer handle this one. I almost died yesterday, Lucy."

Lucy patted my leg. "I'm so sorry. That sounds horrible. I was thinking we should retrace the days of the murder victims and see when they ingested the daffodils."

I gasped. "That's what I was thinking, too."

"Oh, good. You're finally wearing off on me."

"But I'm retired," I explained. "I'm not doing murder anymore."

Lucy rolled her eyes. "Yeah, right."

"I'm serious. Yesterday I had a knife and a gun to my head at once. That's a sign that I need to mind my own business."

Lucy adjusted her beautiful peach-colored dress and ran a hand over her perfectly-coiffed hair. "Gladie, it took me twenty-seven hours of ungodly transportation to get here to help you investigate this killing. Five of those hours were in coach. Coach, Gladie. Do you know what coach is these days? It's like Rikers Island, but without the legroom. Are we clear, darlin'?"

I nodded. "I'll get dressed. Give me ten minutes."

While I took a quick shower and dressed in an above the knee blue sheath dress that Lucy insisted I wear instead of my usual casual outfits, I gave her the entire rundown of the suspects and the latest about Joyce.

"This is a doozy of a case, Gladie," she said, inspecting my room and organizing Spencer's and my stuff on my dresser. "You've never had a poisoning before. It's elegant. Stylish."

I thought back to what Frank had told me about poisoning. Women did it. That would line up with Cynthia and Detective Foxy Bossy. But I needed to find out how they did it. I needed proof.

Uh oh. I guessed I had come out of retirement.

"We'll have to start at the center of the action," I told Lucy.

She picked up her purse. "I'm ready. Let's get 'em." I opened my bedroom door and stepped out. "Phew," Lucy said. "Good to get some fresh air. It smelled like all the sex in all the world happened in your room, darlin'."

We drove to Tea Time in Lucy's peach Mercedes. I figured the tea shop was the center of all action in Cannes, and besides, I needed coffee.

"Large latte, Ruth, and keep 'em coming," I called to Ruth when we entered.

"Don't you see I'm busy?" she screeched back.

"Ruth seems like she's in a good mood," Lucy noticed. "I wonder what's wrong."

"She's smiling," I said, surprised. "I didn't know her mouth could go up like that."

We sat at a table and waited for our coffee. Ruth didn't seem to be in a hurry. She was wiping down the bar with a wet cloth, as if she was trying to get through the layers of varnish. And she was smiling.

"What is that woman smiling at?" Lucy asked.

There were about seven stools at the bar, but there was only one person sitting there. It was a man in a perfectly tailored suit, his shoulders wide, and his hips narrow. I knew those hips. Those were Bolton hips. Spencer had a pair just like them. They were very good hips. It was Peter, Spencer's brother, sitting on a stool, and Ruth was wiping down the bar right in front of him.

"Is she…laughing?" Lucy asked.

Ruth was laughing. Like a ninth-grade girl who gets attention from the school's quarterback, she giggled and flipped her hair, even though her hair was cut close to her head.

"I can't believe you fixed my ancient freezer like it was nothing," Ruth gushed at Peter.

"It was nothing. The least I could do."

Ruth giggled elaborately. She was digging deep into a crush for Peter.

"She's under the spell," I said.

"What spell?"

"The Bolton spell." There was no cure for it. Once under it, a woman was helpless.

"Bolton? You mean Spencer Bolton? What are you talking about? Oh my. Oh my, my, my, my, my."

Peter turned around on the stool and threw me his four-thousand-watt smile. "Ruth, would you excuse me a moment?" he asked her, and she giggled in response.

"Spencer?" Lucy asked.

"His brother, Peter," I said.

Lucy slapped her chest, as if she was having a heart attack. "There's another one? Oh, my, God is great." She punched me in the arm. "You said you told me everything, Gladie. But you left out the most important thing."

Peter stood over our table. "I hope you don't mind, but I've ordered a round of scones and clotted cream. Lattes all around?"

"I don't mind in the least, darlin'. I love all of those things."

"Peter, this is my friend, Lucy. Lucy, this is Spencer's brother, Peter."

She put her hand out, like she was Anna Karenina. Peter took her hand and bowed. Then, he sat down. "Ruth, I'll take another round, if you don't mind!" he called. This time, Ruth loved being yelled at across the shop. She pulled out a fancy bottle with a mysterious brown liquid and practically skipped to our table, where she topped off Peter's latte with the brown juice.

He took an appreciative sip and closed his eyes. "Ruth, I love any woman who doses my coffee." He put an arm around her lower back and pulled her in close to his side.

Ruth giggled and flipped her short hair, again. "Oh, Peter," she said. "I could be your mother."

I coughed. "You mean great-grandmother," I muttered under my breath, but Ruth heard me and shot me a look that could kill.

"I'll get you your latte," she growled and pulled away from Peter.

Lucy put her elbow on the table and rested her chin on her hand. "So, Peter, tell me everything about you. Are you here visiting Spencer?"

"Yes, and other things," he said, winking at me.

"He's looking into Mike's murder, too. Mike might have been a spy," I told Lucy.

"You told me that you had updated me on everything," she spat at me between her teeth. I shrugged my shoulders.

"The spy thing seemed like it was inconsequential to me," I said.

"Really?" Peter asked. "Tell me your reasoning."

"Okay. Okay. I'm sorry. I don't mean to tell you your business. You're probably right."

"No, Gladie," Peter said, touching my hand. "I want to

know your reasoning."

"Are you joking?" I asked. "You want to know my opinion?"

Peter smiled. He had a great smile. Boy, the Bolton genes were off-the-charts, like they were created in a designer studio or something. He had a drop dead, hubba-hubba, hunkmobile, muscles-r-us body, but more than good-looking, he moved like an athlete mixed with a ballerina. Smooth, quick, and agile. Peter was an enigma wrapped in whatever one wrapped an enigma in, but whatever it was, it made Peter mysterious. A tall, dark mysterious stranger, but nevertheless, Peter was wide open and friendly to everyone. The perfect best friend. And he wanted to know my opinion. How weird.

"I'm not joking. Spencer told me about your talents." I arched an eyebrow. "Not those talents. The Miss Marple talents. You have quite a reputation. I'm impressed."

Lucy elbowed me. "I told you," she said to me and turned toward Peter. "Gladie has a real talent for death. If there's a stiff in a ten-mile radius, she'll find it. She's like one of those corpse dogs the police have, darlin'. And then once she finds them, she finds the killer. And sometimes the killer finds her! That's why I came back early. I like to watch her in action and be part of it."

Peter nodded appreciatively. "So, tell me, Gladie, why is the spy thing inconsequential?"

I was blushing. My face was hot. I wasn't used to being complimented. "Well, you see, it's the daffodils that have me questioning the spy thing," I said.

"Spies can kill in a million different ways," Peter said, and I got the impression that he was speaking from experience.

"So, why pick daffodils?" I asked. "A spy could have used anything. Umbrellas, killer dog, zombie. But daffodils are a local flower. It's what this town does every year at this time. Daffodils. So, for me, this murder screams local. A local murder."

Which didn't make sense. But none of it made sense.

Peter seemed to think of what I said for a minute. "I think you're right, Gladie."

"I am?"

"I think my job here is done, not that I have a job, not that I'm doing a job, and if you say I'm doing a job, I'd have to kill you," he said with his beautiful smile. He took a sip of his spiked coffee and took a bite of his scone. He made eating and drinking look pornographic, but when a man was so good looking, brushing his teeth became pornographic.

"Let's let him kill us," Lucy whispered to me. "I think it might be fun."

Peter stood and threw down a wad of bills onto the table. "Unfortunately, that means that I have to go. There's a Bombardier Global 7000 plane with my name on it, sitting on a runway close to here, and it's itching to take off."

He buttoned his jacket. Then, he took my hand and kissed it gently. Lucy stuck her hand out, and he kissed it, too. Ruth skipped to our table.

"You're not leaving, are you?" she asked, desperate.

"I wish I could stay. This would be my go-to place every morning. If I got up in the morning, that is. I don't usually like life before noon. But I made an exception today."

Peter winked at Ruth, and she smiled like her whole world had turned into cotton candy.

"I wish we could have more men like you in this ass-backward town," she said, wistfully.

The door to Tea Time opened, and Uncle Harry walked in with a tall goon. He wasn't actually my uncle, but he liked me to call him that. He had also just recently married Lucy. Uncle Harry was a short man with no neck, and he worked in a dubious business where men in bad suits smoking cigars was de rigeur.

"Lucy, my beauty, I can't find my skivvies. I'm walking around with my shlong swinging between my pants legs," he announced as he reached our table.

"Did you check your suitcase, darlin'?" Lucy asked her new husband, obviously delighted by his presence. Lucy had fallen hard for Harry. It was a real love match, and I had never seen her happier.

"Sonofabitch," Harry shouted, looking at Peter. "Is that

you, Peter?"

Peter slapped his hand against Harry's and gripped it in a handshake. "Harry, great to see you. I never thought I'd see you in a tea shop."

Harry shrugged. "I got domesticated, and now I can't find my drawers. What the hell are you doing here? The last time I saw you, fifteen guys were doing karate chops at your head. I thought you would be dead and buried by now."

"It was twenty guys," Peter corrected. "And let's just say, they're not doing karate chops, anymore."

Harry smacked Peter's back. "I owe this man my life and a few bucks, too," he told Lucy. "Only man who can outdrink me, outfight Spencer, and outspell my sixth-grade teacher. Most guys with his skills sets don't have much upstairs, but this guy went to Oxford. Oxford. Can you believe it?"

"Actually, I went to Cambridge," Peter said.

"That's good, too, right?" Harry asked.

Peter shrugged. "Good beer."

"Good beer," Harry repeated, laughing and slapping Peter's back, again. "I love this guy."

"Hey man," Harry's goon said to Peter, holding up his right hand. "Look, Peter, the pinky's held after all this time. Thanks for the medical care. You really saved me in Yemen."

Peter shook the goon's hand with the intact pinky. "It's nothing that the average Joe wouldn't have done for you, Roscoe. And let's keep the Yemen thing under wraps, okay?" he said with a congenial smile.

The goon blushed. "Sure thing, Peter. Whatever you say. And I owe you one."

It was like a Goodfellas reunion in a tea shop.

Peter crouched down and whispered in my ear. "I'm throwing it back to you, Miss Marple. I'm off to save the world...again. So, here's a gift for my new favorite woman: Mike was at Bird's Hair Salon on the day he was killed. Thought you'd like to know." Peter stood up and faced his adoring fans. "I'm going to say goodbye to my little brother, and then I'm outta here," he said and then he was gone.

Like Batman.

We all stared at the door for a minute, waiting, perhaps, for him to change his mind and grace our presence once again. But he didn't return. The international man of mystery had left the building.

Uncle Harry drove away with the goon to buy underpants, and Lucy and I walked over to Bird's salon. Bird was the queen of upkeep in Cannes. She adhered to the religion of beauty maintenance and gave my grandmother a house call once a week to do her hair and other necessities. Recently, Bird had had a run-in with a bad diet and had now sworn off all diets.

"What the dickens is happening over there?" Lucy asked as we approached the salon. There was a group of people on the sidewalk outside, and they were yelling at each other.

"It's the Daffodil Committee," I told her. "There's a flower controversy this year."

"What a crazy town. I can't believe I left on that honeymoon. What was I thinking? They don't have this stuff in Thailand."

Meryl, the blue-haired librarian, was among the group on the sidewalk. "What's going on?" I asked her.

"The Committee has split into two sides. There's the white side and the yellow side," she explained. "It's the Civil War all over again. Brother against brother. No uniforms yet, though."

"Isn't the daffodil show tomorrow? Is it still going to happen?" I asked.

Meryl shrugged. "Cannes has hosted the daffodil show since my grandmother was a little girl, but I'm not sure we're going to have one this year. Morris won't let one white daffodil in, and the white daffodil supporters say there'll be no show without some white."

"What do you want?" I asked. "White or yellow?"

"I don't know. I just like the margarita bar after the show. Real lime. Delicious."

Lucy and I pushed our way past the flower feuders into the salon. Inside, everything was different. I mean, different than the salon used to be. Bird's salon used to be a utilitarian shop with nicely painted walls and pictures of perfectly coiffed people on them.

Now, Bird's salon looked more like an ashram. Like the Beatles were going to walk in at any moment. Brightly colored fabric was draped on just about every surface, and the employees were dressed in saris. Indian music was being piped in through speakers, and psychedelic lightbulbs had replaced the normal ones.

Besides the way she was dressed, Bird was exactly the same. She had lost the weight she had gained the month before, and she was doing the hair of three clients at once. Not only did she do good hair, she did it fast and didn't sit down for twelve hours a day.

My timing was perfect. I had arrived when her three clients of the moment were all in various stages of getting their gray dyed. So, Bird had a moment to talk with me.

"I have three minutes, Gladie," she told me. "I have my meditation and yogic centering to do before I pull through Sybil's color."

"You redecorated," I said.

"It's my new diet. The Diet of Zen. I've already lost ten pounds. You should try it, Gladie."

I sucked in my stomach. Eating with my grandmother had given me a mushy middle. "I was thinking of watching what I ate," I told her.

She put her hands on my cheeks and looked deep into my eyes. "It's not about what you eat. It's about what's eating you. You need to clear your chakras and manage your chi."

It sounded painful.

"Bird, did you join a cult?" Lucy asked.

"No, it's a diet. A new way of life. Listen, Lucy, when's the last time you saw a fat yogi?"

She had a point.

"Gladie, let me know when you want to start, and I'll give you the rundown," Bird said. "Okay. Gotta get back to Sybil."

"Wait a second," I said. "I have a question. The man who was murdered. I hear he was in here the day he died."

"That jerk?" Bird asked.

"That's the one."

"Yep. He wanted a shave. I do that, too, you know."

"Did he say anything, like that someone wanted him dead?" Lucy asked.

"He was a jerk. He said my salon was for pussies. I shaved

him, anyway."

"That's it?" I asked, disappointed.

"That's it," Bird said and walked back to pull through Sybil's color. We followed her.

"Did he eat anything?" Lucy asked. "Like flowers? Did he eat any flowers?"

Bird stopped what she was doing and stared at Lucy. "Did he eat any flowers? No. He didn't even eat a hamburger, and I'm pretty sure he would have eaten beef before he chowed down on flowers. Damn it. I forgot to meditate."

"Did he mention anybody while he was here?" I asked.

"Nope," Bird said. "I mean, nobody except for that new woman in town. The retired one."

My skin prickled, and blood raced in my veins. "You mean Cynthia?" I asked.

"That's the one."

Lucy and I exchanged looks. Cynthia had spoken to Mike on the day he was killed, before I had taken her to the conference to meet her match. That meant she had known Mike. The image of her bumping into him right before he died flashed through my mind.

The idea that my match was a killer threw me. Being a matchmaker was a very personal thing. I was helping people fulfill their hearts' desires. Now I was faced with the fact that Cynthia had lied to me and could have been involved in a man's murder. I felt betrayed.

I was so deep in my own thoughts that I didn't notice when the Daffodil Committee worked its way into the salon. They were loud and angry, and it turned out that their anger was directed at Sybil, who was getting her color done. It turned out that Sybil was ground zero for the white daffodil movement. I should have known because she had a bouquet of them in her lap and white daffodils painted on her palazzo pants.

"Get back!" Bird shouted at the flower people.

The head of the committee, Morris, pushed his way to Sybil. "Saboteur! J'accuse!" he yelled, pointing his finger at her with his arm outstretched.

"White daffodils are now. Yellow daffodils are stale. They're the past. Hail to the future!" she announced from her chair.

"How dare you!" Morris yelled, affronted. His face had turned red, and he was sputtering when he talked.

Sybil raised her bouquet over her head in a threatening gesture. "Get back or I'll bouquet your ass, Morris. I'm through with taking your yellow daffodil shit. You've been a bully for years, but now we're taking back the power. Power to the white daffodils! Power to the white daffodils!"

"Wha...uh...nah...aagh!" Morris burst out and in one

swoop of his arm, grabbed Sybil's bouquet and threw it into the waxing area of the salon.

"Okay, that's it," Bird announced. She opened a drawer and took out a gun. "Back away from my customer, Morris, or I'll shoot you full of holes!"

"You wouldn't dare," Morris growled.

"Oh, wouldn't I? Nobody gets in between me and beauty!" Bird growled back. She pointed the gun at Morris.

"Now, Bird," I said, but it was too late. Bird let loose and started shooting.

CHAPTER 11

You know me, dolly. I think it's always time to fall in love. But sometimes it's not. Sometimes before you get the answer, you got to get to working. Shoe leather. Wear out those feet, taking the steps to get to where you want to go. Actually, that's a good lesson for life, too. Shoe leather. Look at me, bubbeleh, I'm a philosopher! Call me the Dalai Lama.

Lesson 94, Matchmaking advice from your
Grandma Zelda

"Bird, you're Zen! You clear your chakras and manage your chi!" I shouted, but she continued shooting.

Lucy and I hit the deck. Half of the Daffodil Committee ran from the salon, but none of the salon's customers budged. They continued getting their hair done, getting pedicures, manicures, and waxes, like nothing was out of the ordinary. Like it was a normal day at the beauty shop.

Bird kept shooting. I didn't want to watch, but Lucy peeked.

"My God, Morris is bulletproof," Lucy gasped.

I looked. Bird had shot Morris at least three times, but he wasn't hurt. "Oh, geez, she's shooting blanks," I said.

Lucy and I got back up. "You're shooting blanks," Morris growled at her.

"Of course, I am," Bird said. "I'm trying to get you to lay off my customer, but I'm not psychotic. I keep my gun handy with plenty of blanks to shoo off creeps like you."

"But…" Morris began. Bird cut him off with another round of gunfire. It was an elaborate way of kicking someone out of her place. But if nothing else, it was a hell of a racket, and dejected, Morris gave up trying to talk to Sybil.

With the argument over and the shooting done, Lucy and I walked outside with him.

Lucy said something, but my ears were ringing from the gunfire.

"What?" I yelled. She moved her lips again. I could make out something about weird and crazy.

I nodded. "It sure was crazy!" I yelled.

"What?" she shouted back.

The three of us rubbed our ears. Finally, I could hear, again.

"That woman is batshit crazy," Morris complained. "I wish she would go back to a high carb diet. She was a much nicer woman when she was eating potatoes."

I wished she would eat potatoes, too. Dieting sucked balls. If I couldn't eat potatoes, I might have shot people with blanks, too.

"What?" Lucy shouted.

"Crazy!" Morris yelled back at her, moving his finger in a circle by his head.

"What?"

It occurred to me that I had the daffodil expert in front of me, and I could get information from him. "Morris, do you know anyone who does things with daffodils?" I asked. "Chemistry sort of things with daffodils?"

"Are you talking about the poison? You're the third person to ask me. Cops keep trying to tarnish the reputation of this beautiful flower. I'll tell you what I told them: Nobody who loves daffodils would ever use them to kill a person."

"What?" Lucy shouted.

Luckily, five minutes later, Lucy could hear again. She drove us to Cynthia's house because we planned to grill her on what she had been doing with Mike on the day of his murder.

Lucy parked her Mercedes in the driveway. It was empty, with no sign of Cynthia's car, which made me nervous. We got out and rang Cynthia's doorbell. Nothing. No answer.

"Keep a look out," I told Lucy.

"Why? What are you going to do?"

I took my lock picks from my purse. "We're going to do some snooping. I'm tired of minding my own business and playing nice."

"Holy crap. You can pick locks? You're amazing!" She gave me a hug, and I hugged her back before returning to my lock picking. It took me less than a minute to open the door. I had a real gift for breaking and entering. At least I had a fallback career if the matchmaking didn't work out.

Inside, the house looked the same. There were no dirty dishes in the sink and no sign of life in the house. "Gladie, come on in here," Lucy called from Cynthia's bedroom. "Look at this," she told me when I walked into the room. She had opened the closet. "Nothing but one pair of stirrup pants and a polyester shirt with two-inch-thick shoulder pads. Gladie, Cynthia has taken a powder."

I searched her drawers and the medicine chest in her bathroom. Yep. Everything important was long gone. Cynthia had left, and she probably went with Sidney Martin, the man I matched her with.

What a coincidence.

We went back into Cynthia's kitchen. Since it was lunchtime, and we didn't think that Cynthia would miss some ham and bread, we made sandwiches with chips, grapes, and Diet Coke.

"I don't think they left on their cruise, yet," I said, munching a barbecue potato chip. "They just met."

"The killers are on the lamb," Lucy said thoughtfully, taking a bite of her ham sandwich. "Fleeing the authorities on a cruise. That's nice for them."

I looked for dessert and came up with a half-empty package of Oreos. The dead end was frustrating for me. Cynthia was my last clue, and now she had vanished. It was looking like the Mike Chantage murder was never going to be solved.

"I wish she had ice cream," Lucy said, opening the freezer. "Nope. Nothing but fish sticks and frozen peas. Damn. We should have had the fish sticks, Gladie. That would have hit the spot."

There was a loud knock on the door, and we both jumped.

"Oh lawd, they came back from their cruise," Lucy whispered, her eyes wide with fear.

"They wouldn't knock on their own door," I said. I put my finger against my lips and shushed her. I tiptoed to the front door and peeked through the peep hole, just as there was another loud lock.

It was Detective Pitbull Pretty.

Shit.

I tiptoed back to Lucy.

"Cynthia Andre, open up, or I'll break down the door!" Detective Big Mouth Panties yelled.

"What's happening?" Lucy whispered.

"We're going to be arrested. I'll probably get the needle. Is the death penalty still legal in California? Who am I kidding? She'll probably shoot me, herself. It's Spencer's new detective, and she hates me. She's going to shoot me. She's going to beat me to death. Tase me to death. All kinds of things that wind up in death. My death, Lucy. My death."

Lucy handed me my Diet Coke. "Drink," she ordered. "You're getting splotchy and sweaty."

I gulped it down, but I didn't feel better. The knocking and yelling on the other side of the door was continuing and getting louder. I grabbed a handful of Lucy's dress.

"We have to get out of here," I whispered. "She'll arrest me."

"Maybe we can talk our way out of trouble."

"Breaking and entering and eating ham under false circumstances," I counted on my fingers. "I'm not a lawyer, but I know that amounts to at least ten years. I've already worn an orange jumpsuit, Lucy, and I don't look good in it."

Lucy blinked. "Orange isn't my color, Gladie."

"Grab your purse."

We tiptoed through the house and made it into Cynthia's bedroom just as the front door was busted open.

"Is she allowed to do that?" Lucy whispered to me.

"Come on," I urged her. As quietly as I could, I opened the window, praying that Detective Boobs Bitch took her time with the rest of the house before she made her way to the bedroom.

I laced my fingers together and crouched down. "Come on," I whispered. "I'll hike you through."

"You'll what?"

"Come on. Hurry."

Lucy took her heels off and tossed them through the window. She put one of her perfectly pedicured feet on my hands and put her hands on the windowsill, and I heaved ho my friend. She sailed through the window, and I heard her hit the other side with an oomph. I peeked through the window to see Lucy roll off the hedges and onto the ground. She stood and gave me the OK signal. It was my turn, but I didn't have anyone to heave ho me. I looked around for a chair, but Cynthia didn't have chairs in her room.

That's when I heard Detective Doom Va Va Voom coming down the hallway. I had to think quickly.

Unfortunately, I wasn't thinking quickly. In fact, I wasn't thinking at all. But I was panicking like a champ. I spun around in a circle, hoping something would come to me, but I was blinded by images of me behind bars. She was coming closer, and I was standing in plain sight, easy to be shackled and thrown into a dungeon.

Just as she was about to enter the room, I ducked under the bed. Yes, it was a stupid thing to do. Yes, hiding under the bed was the number one cliché in hiding. The first place she would look was under the bed. I was sure that she was going to find me. I prepared myself for my eventual incarceration: Bad lighting. Pooping in front of others. Being the sweet honey of a woman named Brad. I didn't want any of those things. Especially the bad lighting. I had a yellow undertone to my skin, and fluorescents made me look jaundiced. I didn't know what jaundiced meant, but I knew it was bad and very unattractive, and that would piss Brad off, and… Oh, crap. Pre-incarceration was driving me crazy. I was one dust bunny away from losing my marbles.

And there were a lot of dust bunnies under Cynthia's bed. She had a lot left to be desired in the domestic goddess arena.

"Cynthia, you bitch," I heard Detective Nasty Britches say.

I watched her shoes, as she walked to the closet. "You took a powder. You hit the road. Well, you can run, but you can't hide. I'll track you down if it's the last thing I do."

Wow, there was very little difference between her and a 1980s-adventure movie script.

She sat down on the bed, and it sagged into my back. I held back a moan of pain, as all of the air was squeezed out of my lungs. For a woman with six-percent body fat-- except for her plentiful, perfect breasts-- she sure weighed a lot.

"I'm tired of this pissant town," Detective Adorbs Asshole grumbled. "Bunch of moronic, ingrate incompetents. First that idiot Burger woman who can't stop herself from butting in like an old lady at a bridge tournament, then a bunch of rotten, so-called top cops getting murdered. And now this. This. This, this, this, middle-aged nobody getting one up on me."

She stood up and kicked the bed. Then, she systematically went bonkers through the room, ripping apart every piece of furniture. She pulled out the drawers and tossed them across the room. She flung off the lamp shades. She cut open the mattress with a knife. She looked everywhere except for under the bed.

Go figure.

She screeched some more, mainly cursing "The Burger Woman", which I thought was totally unfair because I had barely butted into her investigation, if she didn't count me breaking and entering and hiding under the bed.

I wished she would hurry up with her rampage because my boobs were getting mushed in a very uncomfortable way. I also had already snorted more than my share of dust bunnies, and I was fairly certain that a spider was crawling up my shirt.

It was all I could do not to scream. If Detective Hotsy Bitchy didn't hurry up, I was going to have to escape from under the bed and try to talk my way out of this mess, even though I didn't think that was possible. She was out for blood. My blood.

Finally, she moved on to the next room. I could hear her turning Cynthia's house into a shambles. She was going at it with a vengeance, all the time talking to herself. It was now or never. Time to escape. While she was in the kitchen tossing plates as if it was a Greek wedding, I decided to get out of there. I was going to use every athletic fiber of my being to climb out the window, meet up with Lucy, and speed away in her luxury automobile before we were caught and dragged off to our doom.

I made my move, but I couldn't move. There was no moving at all. I tried to get my hands underneath me, but the only underneath me there was rust-colored shag carpet from 1966. I tried to wiggle out, but I couldn't wiggle. I tried to shift my legs, but I couldn't shift. I was totally out of action verbs under the bed.

I was stuck.

I needed a jar of Crisco to get out of there. I was wedged in like a sardine but worse.

And I had to pee.

I was stuck forever. I was going to die there. I was gripped with claustrophobia and whatever phobia it was to be afraid of being stuck under a bed.

I was in a quandary. If I cried out, Detective Rat Gorgeous would save me, but then she would shoot me and throw me into the slammer. If I didn't cry out, I would die under the bed, and that wasn't the way I wanted to die.

Actually, I was still up in the air about how I wanted to die, but I was leaning toward getting bonked to death by Spencer while eating Malomars.

I didn't cry out. I focused on trying to breathe while Cynthia's house was tossed. Then, somehow, I fell asleep and dreamed that I was eating Malomars while Spencer was sucking my toes. All in all, it was a really good dream.

"Are you kidding me?"

"Keep sucking," I moaned.

"This one takes the cake."

I opened my eyes and saw Spencer's head as he crouched down and looked under the bed. "What's happening?" I asked.

"I think you're hiding under the bed. Not your bed. Not my bed. A stranger's bed."

"What are you talking about?" I said, forgetting where I was. Then, I tried to move and it all came back to me. "Oh, Spencer, thank goodness you're here! Please save me. I'm stuck. Wait a second. Is you-know-who here?"

"Who?"

I clamped my mouth closed. I didn't know how much Spencer knew about my situation. With one move, he threw the bed onto its side, freeing me.

"How did you get stuck?" he demanded, giving me a hand up.

I dusted off my clothes. "I'm not sure. I got in just fine, but then I must have swollen up like my feet do when I wear tight shoes."

Spencer stared at me, unblinking, for a moment. Then he blinked. "No. What I mean is, what were you doing under the bed? What were you doing in Cynthia Andre's house?"

"What was I doing under the bed? What was I doing in Cynthia Andre's house?"

Spencer squinted at me, as if I was hard to see. "Pinky, why are you repeating everything I say?"

"Why am I repeating everything you say?"

He pointed at me. "There. You did it, again. Why are you doing that?"

"Why am I doing that?"

"Stop it, Pinky. Are you trying to make me crazy?"

"Am I trying to make you crazy?"

It was a weak effort to try and get him off the scent. I didn't know what else to do. My goose was cooked.

Spencer shook his head at me, like I had gotten a word wrong in the local spelling bee. He shrugged his shoulders, as if he had decided something. Without preamble, he grabbed me and kissed me hard, like it was 1917, we were at the train station, and he was going off to war. Everything spun around as our tongues touched, and I melted against his hard body. Spencer was in charge. My body, my self, and my heart, were totally his while he kissed me. When he finally stopped, he held me up since I had gone boneless, slumped against him like a newborn baby.

"That's called a reboot, Pinky," he said, more than a little pleased with himself. "Now, tell me what you were doing here."

I was about to tell him everything. In that moment, I would have even told him my weight. He was the kissing Gestapo. He could make me talk with one slip of his tongue.

I opened my mouth to spill the beans when Lucy rushed into the room, pushed Spencer out of the way, and hugged me, hard. "Oh, darlin', I thought you were done for. Done for! When I understood that you were trapped and that woman was a loony bird, I hid behind a tree and called Spencer. Thank goodness she didn't find you."

"Who? Who didn't find you?" Spencer asked.

The effects of his kiss had worn off, and my brain's survival instinct was restored. But even so, I was tired of Spencer thinking his hot new detective was so hot. I mean, she was hot, but she was crazy. And she hated me. Nobody hated me. Even people who tried to kill me didn't hate me. Why did she hate me?

"Your new detective. Terri Williams. She's looney tunes. Look what she did to this place," I said, avoiding any mention of my breaking and entering.

"Williams did this? This?" he asked looking around the room. It was a disaster.

"Serves you right," Lucy said.

"What does that mean?" Spencer asked her.

She pointed at him. "You know exactly what I mean."

I knew exactly what she meant. Spencer shouldn't have hired a woman who was better looking than I was, but we couldn't say that because it was a betrayal to womanhood.

"I don't understand what's going on. Why were you two here?"

"So, get your detective under control," I said, again avoiding any explanation of what I was doing there. "She's a danger to the public and should probably not be here."

Lucy put her arm around me. "Preach," she said with every

ounce of southern belle in her body.

I tried to avoid Spencer's eyes, but they were like magnets, drawing me into his gaze. We locked eyes. "Gladys," he growled, menacingly.

"Don't call me Gladys," I squeaked.

Spencer was all man, even when he was acting like he was four years old. He was stacked in the testosterone department, and when he was an aggressive he-man, he was a really aggressive he-man. Lucy dropped her arm and stepped back out of Spencer's range.

"Gladys," he continued, taking a few steps forward, forcing me to back up until I was against the wall. He put his hand on the wall over my head and leaned in. "Gladys Burger, tell me what you were doing in this house."

"Don't you want to know about your crazy detective?"

His lips touched my ear and when he spoke, his warm breath sent shivers up and down my body. "I don't sleep with my crazy detective. I don't love my crazy detective. I'll deal with her later. I deal with you always. Always. So, tell me why you were in this house."

"Oh, my," Lucy breathed from the other side of the room. I sighed and closed my eyes. Spencer was very good at seduction.

"Well, the thing is…" I started.

Then, my phone rang. Saved by the bell.

I put my finger up in the air and fished the phone out of my purse. "Pinky, call them back later. This is serious," Spencer said, seriously.

"So is this," I said, rolling my shoulders back and standing tall. "I'm a professional."

I was so full of shit.

I answered the phone. "Gladie, it's Larry. Larry Doughy. Do you remember me?"

Did I remember him? The last time I saw him, he had flown out of my car and was hanging over a highway sign, hundreds of feet in the air. He was sort of hard to forget.

"Of course, Larry. Are you okay?" There was a ninety-five percent chance that he wasn't okay. The curse theory was gaining traction, as far as I was concerned.

"They're letting me out, but I need someone to drive me home. Would you mind picking me up?"

I was between a rock and a hard place. Between picking up Larry from the hospital and possibly getting eaten by a dinosaur or whatever other cursed thing could happen or explaining to Spencer that I broke into a house and stole ham. It was an easy decision.

"I would be happy to, Larry. I'll pick you up in fifteen minutes," I said and hung up. "Gotta go," I told Spencer and signaled to Lucy to hightail it out of there.

We ran to the car without looking back. "Hurry!" I urged Lucy. She unlocked the car and started it up.

"You know, you're going to be alone with him tonight at your house," Lucy said, reasonably, as we drove away.

"I'm hoping by then he'll be focused on his detective."

"That woman is nuts," Lucy said. "But she's got a bangin' bod. I peeked through the window and saw her. She looks like she hopped off a cover of Vogue, but you know, in bad clothes."

Lucy dropped me off at home, and she went to meet Harry. I drove to the hospital to pick up Larry. It took a couple of hours to wait for him to get through the paperwork. He was wearing a boot for his broken toe, and his spirits weren't particularly high. I felt guilty, even though I wasn't the one who had cursed him. I didn't even have a Twitter account.

"You want me to take you to dinner?" I offered. "You're probably hungry, unless you want to get home right away."

Larry's face brightened. "I could go for a pork chop, and I know a place. I'll treat."

That sounded perfect to me. Larry needed to stop at the bank on the way to the restaurant. Since his ATM card was lost in the bridge incident, he needed to go inside the bank. Luckily, we arrived just before it closed. I opened the door to the bank, and Larry limped inside.

While he waited in line, I remembered Cynthia's check that she had given me. I had forgotten to deposit it. I fished the envelope out of my purse and opened it. Inside was a check for four hundred dollars, which was the easiest money I had ever made. There was a note, too.

"Gladie," it read. "Did you know that Frank Fellows has a degree in botany? Also, Mike Chantage loved oatmeal cookies."

I turned the note over, but that was all that was written on it. No admission of guilt from the escaped murderers, if they were really guilty. It was a strange note. She was pinning the blame on Frank, and hinting that he killed Mike with oatmeal cookies. Perhaps Frank had brought them from home? Or had he slipped away to bake poisonous cookies in a borrowed kitchen somewhere? There were so many suspects, but I wasn't any closer to figuring out who done it. I put the note back in my purse and signed the back of the check.

As I waited in line, I looked around. Larry and I weren't the only ones who were banking at the last minute. Frank Fellows, Leah Wilder, Detective Bangin' Bod, and Arthur Fox, the plane crash survivor, were all there. Frank and Leah were each being served by bank tellers. Arthur Fox was sitting at a desk with the bank manager, and the detective was waiting to go into the safety deposit box room. Luckily, she didn't see me, and nobody else seemed to notice me, either.

I figured it was kismet to see Frank at the moment that I had read the note about him. I put the check back in my purse and positioned myself between him and the exit. It was perfect timing to interrogate him about his college degree.

Someone tapped my shoulder, and I turned around. It was a bank employee. "Can you step this way, miss?" she asked.

"What way? Where? What's the matter?"

"Nothing, but we need you to come this way."

She walked ahead of me into a small room with a thick, safe-like door. "Would you wait here?" she asked.

"I guess so," I said. I didn't know what was happening. I hadn't been overdrawn in a couple of weeks. As far as I knew, my account was in the black. But ever since I had moved to Cannes, I had been in trouble with my bank more often than not. I guessed whatever was happening now was bad because they had stuck me in a side room for privacy.

I was surprised when Larry walked in, too. "I got the money," he said. "Things are looking up. I really could go for that pork chop. What are you doing in here?"

"I was told to wait in here. I don't know what this room is."

"It's the back of the ATM machines," Larry explained. He showed me the metal boxes sticking out of the back wall.

"I've never seen the back of them," I said, interested. There was a soft click behind us.

"What was that?" Larry asked.

We turned around. The door was closed. I went to it and tried to open it, but it was shut tight, and we were sealed in.

"Don't panic," I said. "Don't panic!" I said, louder, panicking.

Larry's face turned bright red, and his whole body was shaking. "I think I'm going to panic."

CHAPTER 12

Love is like a breath of fresh air, bubbeleh. When a match meets their soulmate, it's like they're alive for the first time. But sometimes love is smothering. It sucks the breath out of a person. It makes you feel like love itself is taking away your life. I'll give you a hint, dolly. That's not real love. Real love doesn't smother. Real love is like a ride in a convertible on a cool fall day. That's some good air.

Lesson 113, Matchmaking advice from your
Grandma Zelda

"This is bad," Larry said.

It was bad. It was really, really bad. "It's not so bad," I said.

Larry searched the room for an exit after we banged on the door for five minutes with no effect. He put his hands on the walls, touching every inch. "No air. No air. This is bad. This is so bad."

"There's air," I said, clawing at my neck, sure I was going to suffocate to death.

"We're in an airless chamber. I need air! I never learned to swim!"

Were we going to need to swim? I couldn't think clearly. *Think clearly, Gladie. What do you do when you've been locked in an airless chamber with a bank safe door? Think. Think.* It was hopeless. I couldn't think. No thoughts would take form in my brain. It wasn't the first time I had been locked up against my will, but I had always had air before.

Air was good.

I had gotten used to air.

I had the air habit.

I needed air.

"There's plenty of air," I said. "Plenty."

"Our faces are going to turn blue, and our heads are going to blow up," Larry said, still looking for a way out.

That didn't sound good. I was pretty sure it would hurt to have my head blow up.

"This has been a doozy of a day," I said, gasping for air. "You won't believe this, but I was trapped under a bed today."

"That happened to me last Tuesday," Larry said. "I could breathe better there than here."

We sat on the floor in hopes that there was more oxygen down there. That's when I remembered that I had a cellphone in my purse.

"I can call for help!" I announced excitedly, holding my purse up. "Can you believe I forgot about my phone? How could I have forgotten about my phone?"

"Hold the phone away from your face, in case it blows up," Larry suggested.

"Excuse me?"

"It could happen," he said, nodding. "My curse may be contagious."

"Is that possible?"

"I don't know. I'm new to this," Larry said. "But I've never gotten trapped with someone else before. Since I was cursed, it's been a solitary sort of thing."

He had a point. I sort of felt like I was cursed. Damn that Twitter! But on second thought, I figured our current circumstances were less supernatural and more human. There were a slew of people in the bank who could have locked me in the room to die. Like the killer, for example. I had been making the rounds, asking a lot of questions, so it wasn't out of the realm of possibilities for the killer to want me dead.

First things first… I needed to breathe.

"I'll call my friend Bridget," I said. I was running out of people to call for my emergencies, but Bridget hadn't saved me for a while and might want a break from tax season.

When I dug in my purse for my phone, Cynthia's note fell out. "You know what this is, Larry?" I asked. He shook his head. "This is a pretty worthless clue. It says that the first murder victim loved oatmeal cookies."

"Me, too," Larry said. "I had the best oatmeal cookies of my life right before I was cursed, but I can't remember where. At work? No, it wasn't at work. Nope, I can't recall."

I liked oatmeal cookies without raisins. Baked raisins made me gag.

I began to dial Bridget when the door to the room opened suddenly. There was a rush of air inside the room. We were saved. My head wasn't going to blow up. It was a miracle. The best kind of miracle. I hopped up and helped Larry to stand. I turned around to thank my savior and possibly kiss him.

But it wasn't a him. It was a her. The worst of all the hers.

"What the hell are you doing in here?" she screeched.

It was Detective Hottie Sadist. I reminded myself that she didn't know that I had broken into Cynthia's house and had witnessed her rampage. I also reminded myself that I was trying to kill her with kindness.

"My hero!" I gushed, planting a phony wide smile on my face. She didn't smile back.

"I saw you go into this room. Do you know the bank is closed? Were you planning a bank robbery?"

"A bank robbery?" I asked. I went from being a buttinski to being a bank robber? I had really given her a bad impression of me.

"Of course we weren't planning a bank robbery. Who do you think we are? I'm a good person. I'm just cursed. We got locked in," Larry explained. "I'm a log cabin Republican!"

"He's a log cabin Republican," I repeated, as if that exonerated us as bank robbers.

Detective Foul Boobtastic liked that answer, but she still looked at me with suspicion. "I've got my eye on you," she said, pointing at her eye.

"Did you see who locked us in?" I asked her. "Maybe Frank Fellows?"

She caressed the gun on her hip, which gave me the creeps. "Don't butt into police business. You're butting in. Didn't we talk about this before? Don't get on my bad side. You wouldn't like it."

She had a bad side, and this wasn't it?

I wanted to stomp my foot and claw out her eyes. I wanted to defend myself. I wanted her to let me butt in. But I was helpless.

She took all of my power. She held all the cards, not to mention a gun. It wouldn't take much for her to arrest me or worse.

It wasn't the first time I had been blocked when I was snooping, but this was the most frustrating. There were a ton of suspects, with one of them dead and two of them on the lamb. I still didn't have a handle on the victims' days before they were murdered or how they were poisoned. Cynthia was hinting about oatmeal cookies, but Cynthia could have been the killer. So, why should I believe her? I was no closer to solving the mystery than the day Mike Chantage was murdered.

And now Detective No Cellulite Beelzebub was preventing me from finding out. There was a revving of my determination motor inside me, and I knew there was nothing that was going to stop me from solving the mystery and rubbing it in her face the first chance I got.

For now, though, I had to play dumb. I was good at playing dumb. I had a lot of experience.

"I'm so sorry. I won't butt in again," I said, still smiling. I took Larry's hand and left the room in a hurry. The bank was dark, and the bank manager stood at the front door with his key ring in his hand, waiting for the last stragglers to leave. We were the last stragglers.

"This was your last chance," Detective Cruel Boobs yelled at us as we left. "If I catch you anywhere around this case again, I'll arrest you. Don't think I can't!"

Larry and I left the bank and got into my car. "Boy, the

hot lady sure is mean," Larry said.

She sure was, and I wouldn't put it past her to have killed Mike and Joyce. In fact, I wish she had killed them so she would be the one in prison.

I put the key in the ignition and started the car.

"Where are we going?" Larry asked.

"I have an errand to do before we go to dinner."

"Okey dokey."

I had a burr under my saddle. My hackles were up. I was a dog with a bone. I was raring to go. I had been stopped at every juncture, but that only served to make me more determined.

I had decided to finally figure out who the murderer was. I wasn't going to stop until the mystery was solved. First up was Frank Fellows. He was one of the three remaining conference participants and one of the two left in Cannes. He had a degree in botany and would have known about daffodils. And he had a juicy motive: Mike Chantage had slept with his wife.

Frank was going to tell me what he knew. I was done fooling around. I drove straight to his hotel.

"This is a nice hotel. My cousin stayed here when she visited me with her family last year," Larry explained.

It was the hotel where all of the conference participants were staying. Actually, it was a small, country inn more than a hotel. It was shaped like a large log cabin, surrounded by tall trees. The inn ran the old-fashioned way, with no computer and just a penciled-in guest book with all the names and room numbers of the guests. Luckily, Larry got caught in the automatic doors, which distracted the woman at the front desk just long enough for me to sneak a peek at the book. Frank was in room three.

As soon as Larry was free from the doors, I gave him a signal, and he met me in the hallway, out of sight.

"Whoa, that was a close one," he said. "It was almost the urinal episode all over again, but it only got a couple of my buttons." He pointed at his shirt where two buttons were missing. "Who are we visiting?"

"Frank Fellows."

"Oh, the botanist. Gotcha."

"We need to be careful," I told him, as we walked to room three. "We can't draw attention to ourselves. Just be cool."

Larry tucked his shirt into his pants. "Don't worry about me. I'm real cool."

I knocked on the room's door, and the door swung open. I stuck my head in. "Frank?" I whispered. There was no answer. "Frank?" I called, again. "He's not there," I whispered to Larry. "Come on. Let's check it out."

"Good. I need to give this bum toe a rest," he whispered back to me.

I held the door open, and Larry walked in first. There was a small entranceway with the bathroom to the right. I went into the bathroom and checked it out while Larry walked into the room to sit down and rest his foot.

The bathroom was a mess with wet towels strewn over the floor. Frank had the usual toiletries on the counter: a razor, shaving cream, and a bottle of cholesterol medicine.

"Gladie," Larry called from the room. "Can you come here?"

I stuck my head out of the bathroom. "Larry," I whispered. "You have to be quiet, remember?"

"Sorry," he whispered back. "Can you come here?"

"What is it?"

"You kind of have to see it."

I walked into the room. "Is this the fellow you were looking for?" Larry whispered, pointing at a body on the floor. It was Frank Fellows, and he was dead, stabbed through the eye with a letter opener.

I was a squeamish person. In my life, I had passed out from the sight of bleeding gums. But in the past few months, I had seen my share of death, so I had gotten beyond fainting at the sight of blood. However, I wasn't used to seeing a man with a letter opener through his eyeball. I got dizzy. The room spun around me, and I realized that I had been holding my breath. Quickly, I sucked air, and the room stopped spinning. Somehow, in the midst of my shock and repulsion, I had a moment of clarity. I knew what we had to do.

"Folks are dropping like flies around here," Larry noted.

He was right. With Frank, three of the five conference guests had been murdered. Since they were all considered California top cops, law enforcement had been dealt a bad blow.

"I'm cursed, but at least I don't have a letter opener through my eye."

"Larry," I whispered. "We're going to back out of here very carefully and pretend that we were never here."

I expected him to argue with me and play the good Samaritan, but I guessed being cursed and faced with a dead man who had a letter opener through his eye had made him slightly less good Samaritan and slightly more careful. We had just been threatened with arrest if we got involved, and here we were at the scene of a murder. It looked like we would be the number one suspects if we were caught in the room with poor dead Frank Fellows.

"Okay," Larry said. "He's dead, right?"

"I'm pretty sure he is." He was deader than a doornail. Stiff as a board. "Be careful to not touch anything. No one will ever know we were here."

"Good. I don't want the mean looker cop to know we were here."

"Exactly," I said. "She'll toss us in jail and throw away the key. You didn't touch Frank, did you?"

"Nope. I've watched CSI. I know what I'm doing."

That was fortunate. I didn't want us to leave any trace of us behind. No fingerprints, no hair, no DNA, whatsoever. I wanted to get out of there and get Larry his pork chop without Detective Hubba Hubba Heinous finding out I was ever near poor Frank Fellows' dead body.

Ever so softly, we both took a step backward. As our feet touched the carpet, the ceiling light made a popping noise and it fell, the cord ripped from the ceiling. The light knocked Larry's back as it fell to the floor, throwing Larry off balance. He shot me a horrified look, as he realized that he was going over but was hopeless to stop it.

Larry fell over fast and landed across Frank's torso. Once he was down, he froze in disbelief, and so did I.

"It's okay. It's okay," I whispered. "Just get up carefully and don't touch him."

Larry put his hands on the floor and pushed himself up, but the boot on his foot was caught on the bed frame. He pulled his leg, but he couldn't get it free.

"I'll help," I whispered.

I leaned over his leg and tried to free him, grabbing his boot and yanking. Finally, I got the boot loose with one hard yank, but the bed moved with it, knocking the nightstand and making a potted plant on it come crashing to the floor. The dirt from the plant flew up and over to us, coating Larry, Frank, and me in a fine lawyer of potting soil.

Larry rolled off Frank and sat up. "This is nothing like CSI," he whispered.

"Don't touch anything," I whispered back.

"I don't think it's too bad. I didn't touch him with my hands."

He was right. It actually wasn't too bad. We hadn't touched the body with our fingers, so there weren't any fingerprints. I took a deep breath and willed my heart to slow down. "All right. Let's get up slowly and get out of here."

"Okay," he said and then closed his eyes and opened his mouth. "I'm...I'm...going to..."

Sneeze. He was going to sneeze. The dirt must have gotten up his nose, and now he was going to sneeze. Larry pinched his nose, in an effort to stop the sneeze, but it didn't help. Larry was a big sneezer. He sneezed with his whole body. A little pinch couldn't compete.

"Ah...choo!" He practically exploded with his sneeze.

"Cover your nose! Cover your nose!" I urged, but it was too late. The sneeze went everywhere. There was sneeze all over the room, sneeze all over Frank's body, and sneeze in my open mouth as I told Larry to cover his nose.

"Uh oh," Larry said, looking at Frank.

I thought, quickly. I had to get rid of Larry's sneeze DNA. I went to the bathroom and picked up one of the towels from the floor. I went back into the room and wiped off every surface I could find, including Frank's face, which was wet from the sneeze. I worked quickly, dusting with the towel.

"There," I said, after I had finished. "All done. Now we can go."

"What's that? Blood?" Larry asked.

"Where?"

"There. On the towel. And your hand. And..." He pointed at Frank's face, as blood dripped onto it.

"What the hell?" I said.

"There. It's coming from your hand. You must have cut it on the bed frame."

I inspected my hand. Sure enough, there was a little cut on the side, and it was bleeding all over Frank's body. The towel was bloody, too, which I hadn't noticed before when I had used it to dust the entire room.

"Sonofabitch," I said. "What do they do in CSI when this happens?"

"I don't know. I must have missed that episode."

I wrapped the towel around my hand. The room was a complete mess. We were doomed. Frank was coated in our DNA. He was head to toe doused with Larry's snot and my blood. I was going to jail for the rest of my life. Spencer would stop loving me.

"What're we going to do?" Larry asked.

"Give up. Throw in the towel," I said, looking down at the bloody towel.

"The mean, pretty cop probably wouldn't believe that we just found him here," Larry said, thoughtfully.

"Nope."

"So, we're going to have to do something crazy," Larry said.

"What do you mean?"

"I mean, crazy."

CHAPTER 13

Matchmaking is a wonderful career, bubbeleh. I think of it as my calling. It's not for those who want to kibitz around, believe you me. But even though it's a calling, it doesn't mean that you can't take a break every once in a while. Stop and smell the flowers! If all you do is work, work, work, how will you enjoy the rewards? This business can suck you in and take over your life. The tumelt can make you crazy. So, it's up to you to stop, take a breath, and smell those delicious flowers.

Lesson 67, Matchmaking advice from your
Grandma Zelda

I had been in the shower at home, scrubbing myself down for twenty minutes when Spencer walked into my bathroom. He pushed the shower curtain aside, sat on the closed toilet seat, and watched me, as I loofahed myself with a vengeance.

"This has been the single weirdest day that I've ever had. Ever," he announced.

I squeezed shampoo onto my hand and lathered my hair for the third time since I had gotten into the shower.

"First, I was called over to save my girlfriend, who had gotten stuck under a bed in a stranger's house," he said.

"It was my match's house, not a stranger's," I corrected and began to rinse my hair.

"Then, I had to interrogate my new detective, who seems to be…"

"Unbalanced?" I supplied. "Sadistic? Hyperactive?"

"I was going to say, overeager."

I squeezed conditioner onto my hand and combed it through my hair with my fingers.

"And then I get a call from a local hotel. An inn," he said, and I almost jumped out of my skin, but I managed to hold myself together. "Frank Fellows is dead."

"Really? Another one?" I said and put my head under the water so that Spencer couldn't tell that I was lying.

"I know, right? It's definitely my last conference. I've managed to kill off three top cops. Who would ever want to come to another conference here? Afghanistan is safer. A minefield is safer. But that's not the weird part."

Here it comes, I thought. I peeked out from the water. Spencer was eyeing my body with his usual horny toad self, which was good news for me. It meant that weird or not, nothing had changed between us.

"We get to the inn, and sure enough Frank has been murdered," Spencer explained. "A letter opener through his eye into his brain. Death was probably instantaneous."

I put more soap on the loofah and gave my body another going over. "I guess that's good for Frank," I said.

"But that's not the weird part. I mean, that was weird, but it gets so much weirder."

I knew that it got weirder. I was the reason it got weirder. But I couldn't let Spencer know that. Running out of body to wash, I began to shave my legs.

"Get this," Spencer continued. "We found Frank naked. He was naked in the bathtub. He had been cleaned from head to toe and left to soak in the tub."

I shuddered. I was never going to forget washing my blood and Larry's snot off Frank's naked, dead body. We had stripped him down and dragged him into the tub. Then, we cleaned the room from top to bottom. Martha Stewart would have been happy to eat off any surface in that room after we were done with it.

"The whole room was scrubbed clean, and his clothes and towels were nowhere to be found," Spencer continued.

I hated cleaning, but I had done things with hotel soap that no one had done before. Who knew I had that much elbow grease? It wasn't the first time I had moved a dead body. A couple months before, I had moved a bunch of them, but this time was more up close and personal.

And naked.

"And here's the thing," Spencer said. "He was washed after he was killed."

"Weird," I said, moving to my other leg.

"Stabbed with a letter opener through the eye, then stripped naked and washed, and get this: he had a washcloth placed over his dick."

That had been my idea. Frank had an unusually large penis, and it had distracted me while I was washing him down.

Spencer loosened his tie and ran his fingers through his hair. He looked worn out. "And now I'm down another detective. I'm calling Remington to come back early to take up the slack."

"Wait. What?" I asked. I was still under the shower, but I had run out of things to do, and the water had turned cold.

"Terri Williams is in my holding cell," Spencer said.

What? Detective Foxy Satan was in the slammer? Was it Christmas already?

I turned off the water, and Spencer wrapped a towel

around me, copping a feel while he did. I stepped out of the tub, and Spencer held me close.

"I'm missing something," I said.

Spencer ground his hard how-do-you-do against me. "You've been missing this, but it's here for you, baby. All twelve inches."

"You're four years old."

"Twelve inches," he said rubbing himself against me and continuing to cop a feel.

"How can you be aroused right now? You've been talking about a man with a letter opener through his eyeball."

"Say, 'ball' again. I've got a pair that are yearning for you."

"Your balls are yearning for me after talking about a murder?"

Spencer flung the towel off me, and then his hands were everywhere. Everywhere. Usually that would turn me into a pile of estrogen jelly, but I was in a post-dead-Frank place, and I just couldn't drum up any desire.

"I just watched you take a shower for ten minutes, Pinky. I'm not dead, you know. Come on, give a guy a break. Bring on the noogy machine."

"My noogy machine is on the fritz," I said.

Spencer took a step back. His face was all concern. "But it's never been on the fritz before. It takes a lickin' and keeps on tickin'."

I picked up the towel and wrapped it around my head. "Smooth talker, Spencer."

He followed me out of the bathroom and into the bedroom. "Maybe not a smooth talker, but I'm all kinds of smooth in other ways."

I sat on the bed and put on a pair of Spencer's socks. "When I said I was missing something, I meant about your detective, Terri Williams. Why did you arrest her?"

"Oh, that. I told you today was weird. Frank's hotel room had been washed down, like he was the king of OCD patients, but there was one spot that was missed."

I wracked my brain, trying to think of where I could have missed. I had even cleaned the backs of the paintings and under the mattress. What had I missed?

"Where?" I asked.

"Pinky, you have great lips. Have I ever told you that?" he asked, staring at my breasts.

"Twice. Come on, tell me and then I'll let you feel a boob before we eat. I'm starved. I want macaroni cheese and meatloaf." I needed comfort food. Murder did that to me.

Spencer smirked. "Best lips I've ever known."

"You know, you're not twelve inches. Twelve inches would reach my belly button."

"Pinky, let a guy have his fantasies."

"Okay fair enough," I said. "But tell me what was missed in the clean-up."

"The letter opener handle."

I blinked. "Excuse me?"

"A fresh set of prints, snab dab on the letter opener handle. Terri's. She killed him. Obviously, she's been on a rampage. I'm sort of doubting my hiring abilities now, but she had stellar recommendations. Meatloaf sounds good."

I had forgotten to clean the letter opener handle. That made sense in a way, because I didn't want to touch it. But I wasn't entirely certain that I hadn't cleaned it. Damn Frank's penis for distracting me. Now I didn't know if her prints had been on it before or after we finished our clean-up.

"Did Terri confess?" I asked Spencer.

"No. She said she found him, didn't realize she had touched the letter opener, and then went to the bank. Dumbest story I've ever heard."

"Yeah, dumb," I said, but I thought if she had been guilty, she would have thought up a smarter story. A little voice inside me was telling me that Detective Devil Stacked was innocent.

And I was going to have to prove it.

Damn it.

The next morning, I left the house bright and early. I had called Larry on the sly and asked him if we had cleaned the letter opener handle, but he couldn't remember if we had or not. He told me that he had decided to stay inside until he could find another goat, and I was supportive of his decision.

Across the street from my grandmother's house, a large truck with a crane on it was pulling the plane out of the house it had crashed into. There was a crowd on the sidewalk watching the progress, along with a camera crew from San Diego, filming it for the news. I joined the crowd. It wasn't every day that one could see a plane getting lifted out of a house.

"Powerful shame," one of the spectators said to me.

"Yes," I replied.

"Two innocents off to meet their makers. Well, one of them wasn't so innocent. Johnnie Brinkhammer probably deserved to meet his maker."

"Johnnie Brinkhammer? Did you know him? I'm sorry for your loss."

"Not my loss," he said. "I just know him through the news and the *Real Court* show I watch every night before *Jeopardy*. Didn't you hear about that case? Brinkhammer was up on a murder charge in a small town up north. He was about to go to trial. He had tried to kill his wife, but the hit man killed the wrong woman. Then, Johnnie tried to get away, I guess, but the Lord took him home, instead."

A whole symphony of bells went off in my head.

"Thank you," I said, and kissed him on the cheek.

It took a lot of convincing to get Leah Wilder to open her hotel room door to let me in. When she finally opened, she made me stay an arm's length away from her. She was packing her bags.

"You're leaving?" I asked.

"I haven't eaten in forty-eight hours because I didn't want to be poisoned, and now I have to worry about getting stabbed through my eye," she said by way of explanation.

She wasn't wrong.

"I don't know what the hell is going on here," she continued.

Leah didn't sound like she was the killer, and she was way too nice to stab Frank through the eyeball.

"Leah, you have no clue who's killing everyone?"

"They arrested the detective with the attitude problem and no body fat," Leah said, dumping her clothes into her suitcase without folding them.

"And yet, you're scared about being murdered. You don't think she did it?"

Leah zipped her suitcase closed and gave me a pointed look. "I don't know who did it. I just know I'm getting out of here. Mike, Joyce, and Frank were all jerks, but I'm not sticking around to find out if the murderer wants to kill nice people, too."

I didn't blame her. I wouldn't have wanted to be in her shoes.

"I get it," I said. "Johnnie Brinkhammer."

"Excuse me?"

"Johnnie Brinkhammer. Have you heard of him?"

"No. Is that a suspect."

"No," I said. "He died in a plane crash here. He was supposed to go to trial for murder."

"Sounds familiar, but I don't know him." She closed her suitcase, put it on the floor and wheeled past me. "Good luck," she said and stopped at the door, turning around. "You like to solve mysteries, right?"

"Me? Not really," I lied.

"Since you're one of the last alive, I'll give you some information. The autopsy showed that Mike's stomach had the same thing in it that we all ate at the lunch. But he also had oatmeal cookies in his stomach. He had eaten those, too. But I spent the whole day with him on the day he was killed, and I didn't see any cookies. There. Knock yourself out, and be careful."

It was the first morning in forever that I had forgotten to drink coffee, and now that I had remembered, I was jonesing. Luckily, I wasn't going far from Tea Time. Morris lived close by, and I wanted to see him and ask him a few questions.

It wasn't the best time to visit him. It was the day of the daffodil show, and his house was bedlam, because it was the show's headquarters. I knocked on his door. One of the daffodil ladies answered, and I walked in.

Morris was in the kitchen, holding a clipboard. Daffodil Committee members were walking in and out, and they were all dressed in yellow jumpsuits. "Are you here to volunteer?" he asked me. "We're going to have a wonderful show this year. Wonderful! I've knocked out the white flower people, and it's going to be yellow, yellow, yellow. We're about to deck out Main Street."

The daffodil show was located on Main Street in the Historic District. They flower bombed the whole street, and the show went on all day and evening.

"I'm sorry. I'm not volunteering, but I'll be at the show later. I wanted to talk to you again about the daffodil poisonings."

"That, again?" he asked. "Listen, I've been thinking about it. Daffodils are poisonous, but it's rare that one would kill a man. Usually it just makes them sick. No, it would have to be a powerful dose."

"You mean a person would have to eat a lot of daffodils?"

"That or a distilled essence of the flower's bulb. A concentrated form."

"How would someone get a concentrated form?" I asked.

"A botanist could have that or an enthusiast. I have a big vial of it."

"May I see it?"

Morris was busy, but he was thrilled to have someone so interested in daffodils that they wanted to see his vial of concentrated daffodil liquid. His garage was filled with everything that had to do with daffodils, from the dirt to the flowers to the pots. He opened a cupboard and sifted through a mess of bottles, cans, and bags.

"It was here, but I can't find it. Maybe I put it somewhere else?" he asked himself out loud.

My Miss Marple ears pricked up. "So, it's missing?" I asked.

"No, not missing," he said, touching his chin and looking around the garage. "Misplaced, I guess. Anyway, I have to get back to the show. It can't go on without my leadership."

We walked back into the kitchen. My stomach growled. I hadn't eaten breakfast, or even had a cup of coffee. The kitchen counter was covered in assorted snacks for the volunteers, and one plate caught my attention.

"Morris, I hate to bother you, but are those oatmeal cookies?" I asked.

"Yep. Good ones, too. Help yourself. My tenant made them."

"Who's your tenant?" I asked and crossed my fingers.

"Arthur Fox. The guy who crashed into the house across the street from yours."

CHAPTER 14

I'm old! I'm fat! I have corns! I have credit card debt! I have sleep apnea! I spit when I talk! My vagina is falling out! Dolly, I've heard it all. Everyone has an excuse about why they can't find love. An excuse about why they need to wait until they date. They want to wait until they're younger, thinner, get foot surgery, make more money, get one of those fakakta sleep machines, and braces. In other words, they're never going to date again. It's your job to explain to them that there's a sock for every shoe, a tuchus for every seat, a finger for every nose. Life is not Photoshop. It's not flawless. Life is horseshoes and hand grenades. You understand me, bubbeleh? What I'm saying is that nobody's perfect, that almosts and close enoughs are good enough to find love. So, tell your would-be matches that they need to start from the here and now. Don't wait. Do it, now.

*Lesson 120, Matchmaking advice from your
Grandma Zelda*

Arthur Fox lived in a two-bedroom apartment above a store, a few blocks away from Morris in the Historic District. I was developing a crazy-ass theory regarding him that I was very excited about. If I had been smart, I would have waited for back-up before going to his place to confront him.

But Lucy was getting her roots done, and Bridget was struggling to deduct a veterinarian's collection of porcelain corgis. So, it was just me. Besides, I was antsy to test my theory about Arthur.

He answered his door before I had a chance to knock, which made me wonder if he had been looking through the peephole. "Hi, there," he said. "Gladys, right?"

"Gladie."

"How can I help you?"

He was a short man, probably a couple inches shorter than I. His hair was cut neat and short, and he was wearing a blue chef's uniform, which made sense, since he was holding a large knife in one hand.

"I was wondering if I could talk to you about your catering services for my grandmother's matchmaking business," I said. "We host a lot of events at her house."

Slowly, a smile grew on his face. "Certainly. You want to come in? I'm doing food prep."

Yes, I wanted to come in. I wanted to spy on him, search every nook and cranny of his apartment, and grill him like a rack of ribs.

Inside, the apartment was nothing like I expected. There was a small living room attached to the kitchen, and the only furniture were stainless steel tables, ovens, and the accoutrements of a professional caterer.

Arthur went back to his cutting and chopping. "When do you need me?" he asked.

"Oh, not for a couple months," I lied. My grandmother was a strictly potluck sort of hostess. I couldn't see her paying for salmon and rice. "It's the house across the street from where you crashed."

"I know," he said, looking up at me for a second before returning to his cutting board. "What kind of menu and how many guests?"

"Do you do fried chicken? That would be a big hit. And anything with potatoes. There will probably be about forty people." I was starting to believe my story about needing a caterer, probably because I was starving. I hadn't eaten, yet.

"Fried chicken is easy. Mashed potatoes, too?"

My stomach growled. "That sounds perfect."

"You hungry?" He put a plate of oatmeal cookies in front of me. "Help yourself. I made an extra batch."

I took a step backward, away from the oatmeal cookies. It was doubtful that he had made a batch of poisonous cookies and was trying to kill me, but you can never be too careful. "Thank you, but I'm meeting friends for lunch, and I don't want to ruin my appetite."

It was a terrible lie. Nothing ruined my appetite. I could have eaten the twelve cookies, a rack of lamb, and a side of bacon, and it wouldn't have ruined my appetite. But I had gotten used to being alive, and I didn't want to give that up for an oatmeal cookie.

Not that I thought Arthur Fox was a killer. There were still Cynthia and Sidney out in the wind, and Detective Bitch McBoobface was in prison, and her fingerprints were all over the murder weapon. And Arthur Fox didn't have a motive, as far as I could tell, unless he was a psychotic serial killer.

A bug flew over our heads, and Arthur dropped the knife and caught the bug. "Moth," he explained. "I breed them."

"You mean like *Silence of the Lambs*?" I croaked.

"Exactly like that," he said, walking to one of the bedrooms with his moth. "Except for the skin suit. I haven't made one of those, yet." He turned and winked at me to show me that he was kidding. Still, bugs were a weird hobby, especially for a cook.

I followed him to the other room, which was dark with a wooden cage for his moths. I was getting the creeps, big time, from his place. He returned the one moth in his hand to the cage and turned toward me. "I get the impression that you want to ask me something," he said, his voice low, like the arch villain in a comic book movie.

"I was wondering how you were getting along since you arrived in Cannes. You must be missing your family."

"I love it here. Everyone's been very welcoming. And I don't have any family. It's just me. Why? Do you want to match me?"

I hadn't thought of it, but it was a great excuse for me nosing around, although Grandma wouldn't have liked me lying about matchmaking.

"Sorry. I guess I'm always thinking about business," I lied. I rarely thought about business. I thought about it slightly more often than I thought about changing my toothbrush.

"I'm not on the market. I like my alone time."

"I understand," I said, following him back to the kitchen. "You probably need time to adapt to your new life. Is it different than your old one? I bet Cannes is different from your previous town."

"I find that one life is pretty much like another and one town is pretty much like another. I just mind my business and cook. Now, if you would excuse me, I really have to get to work. Just call me about two weeks out from your event, and I'll organize everything."

Arthur more or less pushed me to the door and opened it. "Bye," he said.

"The plane crash was such a tragedy," I said. "But I'm so glad you came out of it okay."

"It was a miracle."

"Amazing that you were on the same plane with Johnnie Brinkhammer. An escaped murderer. It was like justice from up above. Literally and figuratively."

"I don't know anything about that. I didn't know the guy," he said, his face an unreadable surface.

"One more thing. Did you give oatmeal cookies to Mike and Joyce?"

He smiled ever so slightly. "You might want to do like I do, Miss Burger, and mind your own business." He cocked his head to the side and studied me for a moment. "No, I guess you don't mind your own business, despite what you say. I've heard about you. I heard about you snooping into the old man's death in the house I crashed into. I guess you can't help yourself. Might be wise to try, though. You don't want to get hurt."

He had pushed me out the door, and now he shut it in my face. I stood there for a moment and caught my breath. I smelled my armpit. It smelled fine. So, why were so many people threatening me lately? I was getting it from all sides, and it was just making me more determined to keep going headlong into finding the killer.

Arthur said he had no family, and there were no photos in his apartment. That was convenient for him, and it gave me an idea. I was going to have to go at this through the back end.

I took a sip of my latte and closed my eyes in appreciation. "Ruth, you make the best coffee in the world. You should change this place to a coffee shop."

"Are you trying to get me to beat you to death?" Ruth growled. "We have a deal for you to get free lattes for a year, but we didn't agree that I had to serve you inside my shop."

She had a point. "Sorry, Ruth. Your coffee sucks."

"That's better. Look, your friends are here."

I turned around to see Lucy and Bridget walk in. Despite the warm weather, Lucy was wearing a knee-length, black trench coat and hat. Bridget was wearing a polka-dotted maternity dress, and her curly hair was hanging over her glasses. She looked tired, and she plopped down on a chair at the nearest table.

"Lech has the hiccups, and every time he hiccups, I have to pee. Uh oh, there he goes again." Bridget jumped up and shuffled to the bathroom, quickly, all the while keeping her knees together.

Lucy sat down and gestured to me to sit next to her. "The red fox trots quietly at midnight," she whispered.

"Huh?" I asked.

"Nothing, darlin'. That's my special spy phrase. Mission

completed. I found the information you were looking for."

Lucy handed me a photo. "That's Johnnie Brinkhammer's wife. Her name is Corinne Brinkhammer. After the whole murder-for-hire thing, she moved away. I haven't found her, yet, but I'm on it."

Bridget came back to the table, and Ruth brought her a pot of tea and a tea cup. "You drink this, Bridget. It's good for your bladder. What are we talking about?"

"It's top secret, Ruth," Lucy said. "Gladie is investigating."

"Is that right? Well, I know that woman," Ruth said, tapping the picture with her finger. "Corinne. She lives on a farm up by the pear orchards. She comes down every once in a while for tea and her crotchet club. She's made half of the tea cozies I sell here. I don't have to order them from out of town anymore. The last time I saw her was about three weeks ago, before the plane crash."

Lucy, Bridget, and I looked at the rack of crocheted tea cozies. I was living in two degrees of separation. All roads led to killers, it seemed.

"Do you have her address?" I asked Ruth.

"I can do better than that. I'll drive you there."

There must have been a lot of money in tea, because Ruth

had bought a brand new, fully-loaded, Mercedes all-electric SUV. I rode in the front next to Ruth, and Lucy and Bridget took the back seat. We had to stop twice during the twenty-minute ride for Bridget to pee in the bushes along the side of the road.

"So what are you thinking, Gladie?" Ruth asked me. "My tea cozy lady has something to do with these murders?"

"I think that new bitch cop is the killer," Lucy said. "Her fingerprints were all over the murder weapon."

"I hope she's getting good representation," Bridget said. "On average, women are more poorly represented than men. I should probably find out."

"What about those two who hit the road? My money's on them," Ruth said.

I didn't tell them who my money was on. I had a theory that was pretty far out, and I didn't want to say anything until I was sure about it.

Ruth turned off the main road onto a narrow, gravel one. We drove up higher in the mountains for about five minutes when the road leveled out to a wide plain. Corinne's house was a small ramshackle one with a wraparound porch and surrounded by fields and corrals.

And lots of goats.

"She raises goats," Ruth explained, as she parked in front of the house. "I guess there's money in goats. Who the hell knows?"

"Women have to turn to their own ingenuity and know-how to make a living these days. Can't depend on a man, and we shouldn't want to," Bridget announced. "Boy, I have to pee."

She was the first to get out of the car, and she banged on the front door.

A woman with thick, flowing gray hair, wearing a crocheted sweater, jeans, and rubber boots came from around the house with a goat in tow. "May I help you?" she asked Bridget.

Ruth opened her car door. "Corinne, Bridget has a baby kicking her bladder. Can she use the can?"

"Of course. The door's open, and the bathroom is second door on the left."

Bridget didn't need to be told twice. She opened the door and bolted into the house.

"Are you Corinne Brinkhammer?" I asked her, offering her my hand.

"What can I do you for? Are you looking for a sweater or a goat?"

"I wanted to ask you about your ex-husband, Johnnie."

Corinne sucked air. "I don't want to talk about him. The man tried to have me killed."

Bridget came out of the house. "Men are pigs, but that's because they've been formed by a misogynistic patriarchal society.

It's not really their fault. Oh, shit. I gotta go again."

Bridget ran back into the house.

"Corinne, how about we go inside and have a little chat. I brought my chocolate chip scones," Ruth said, holding up a pastry box.

There was nothing like sugar and carbs to smooth over awkward situations. Corinne let us in, and we sat at her kitchen table, sipping tea and eating scones.

"Why do you want to talk about Johnnie?" Corinne asked. "He's dead and buried."

"And yet you're still scared of him," I said.

"No, I'm not."

"Then, why did you move out to the middle of nowhere with only goats to keep you company?"

"I like goats," she said. "Although, I do get lonely from time to time."

"You should probably just spit it out," Ruth told her. "Gladie has a way of squeezing secrets out of people. That's why so many people want her dead."

She was right. A lot of people had wanted me dead.

Corinne leaned forward and put her elbows on the table. "All right, I'll tell you, but you're going to think I'm crazy."

"Ha!" Lucy barked. "You don't know Gladie very well. She's all kinds of crazy. But in a good way," she added, throwing me a guilty look.

"There was something fishy about that plane crash," Corinne continued. "Too convenient. Johnnie was a snake in the grass. A schemer. I feel better out here with the goats, where he can't find me, if he's still out there breathing somewhere. Although, you're right. I wouldn't mind a little human interaction. I wouldn't mind finding a man who likes goats and doesn't want to kill me."

Holy crap. In the middle of my sleuthing, I had stumbled on the world's easiest match. I knew where Corinne could find love and solve another problem at the same time. But for now, I had to focus on the murder spree.

"Do you have a picture of Johnnie?" I asked.

"God, no."

"Was he a short man?"

Corinne nodded. "A couple inches shorter than you."

Ding. Ding. Ding. I knew who murdered Mike, Joyce, and Frank, and I knew why. But it wouldn't be easy to prove.

CHAPTER 15

Once in a while, I have a blind day. It ain't pretty. I wander around, not feeling as much as normal. Not understanding as much as normal. On those blind days, I think: Life is over. This is the end. I believe this, even though I've had blind days before, and my life is never over. The blind day ends, and then I'm back to your normal Grandma. But in the moment where I don't see, where my third eye is closed, there's fear. Lots and lots of fear. And the fear is stronger than the experience, dolly. It convinces me that it's the end. But from me to you, dolly, I'll tell you: There's no end. Death, love, blind, seeing...there's no end. The story continues.

Lesson 20, Matchmaking advice from your
Grandma Zelda

"I'm not letting a goat into my brand new Mercedes," Ruth insisted.

"It probably won't poop during the trip," Corinne said.

"It *probably* won't poop?" Ruth asked.

"We need the goat, and Corinne needs to come with us," I said.

Lucy grabbed onto Ruth's arms and gave her a little shake. "Ruth, look at Gladie. She's got the Miss Marple thing happening. Look at her eyes. She's got murder twinkle going on. You know she does. It's not the first time. She *knows* something. She's got the killer in her sights. It's now or never. Don't be a wimp, Ruth. This is about justice. Don't put a wrench in the works, or so help me God, woman, I'll tell the whole town that you drink your tea with the tea bag still in the cup."

Ruth's eyes grew wide, and her mouth opened in a big O. "You wouldn't dare," she said, finally, after the shock wore off. "Lucy Smythe, you wouldn't dare! I would never drink a cup of tea with the tea bag still in it."

Lucy poked Ruth in her chest. "Don't push me, old woman. You play ball with the goat in your car, or the whole town will be using your name and Lipton in the same breath. So, help me."

"You're evil, Lucy. Evil."

Lucy adjusted her trench coat and tightened the sash. "I do what I have to. Gladie is about to unmask the culprit, and I don't want you sabotaging her efforts. I came back from my honeymoon so I could watch her in action. I'm going to see her bag the bad guy this time, no matter what, and nobody's going to stop me. You hear me? Tea bag. Tea bag. Tea bag."

It was a standoff between two strong women. Ruth was stubborn as a mule, but she had a reputation to uphold, and no way was she going to let that go. So, in went the goat, which sat on Corinne's lap between Lucy and Bridget on the ride back into town.

Ruth decided to park at my grandmother's house because Main Street had been blocked off to cars for the daffodil show. Grandma came out of the house and walked down the driveway toward Ruth's car as we got out.

"Dolly, I called Larry and told him to meet you at the show," she told me. "I told him to clean up and bring a hammer."

"Thanks, Grandma." I wanted him to meet Corinne and get de-cursed from the goat. I didn't know what the hammer was about, but I figured it could come in handy.

The five of us and the goat walked to Main Street, which was hopping with activity. Morris had outdone himself. The street was a sea of yellow daffodils. The flowers were everywhere. It was gorgeous, and half of the town was there, enjoying the displays.

"Hello there, Gaddie. How ya' doin'?" Meryl greeted me by the outdoor bar. She was already three sheets to the wind and slurring her speech.

"Just fine," I said, looking around.

"Morrish doesn't know this yet, but the white daffodil peeps are on their way to cause touble," she said and closed her eyes.

"Maybe you should slow down, Meryl. Go and rest for a little while."

"I can't rest! I'm the booze taster, and it tastes petty good shoe me!"

She took another swig.

"I better go guard my shop," Ruth said. "These daffodil people get pretty rowdy. Let me know if you need help, Gladie. I've got my Louisville Slugger all set to go."

"I wish I could have a drink," Bridget said. "Is that a taco truck?"

My stomach growled. One chocolate chip scone wasn't enough to hold me over for the whole day. I was starved. So, I gave the go ahead to get some tacos. It was lucky for us because Larry was there, too.

"Hello, Gladie. Careful of the tacos. One almost put my eye out," he said. "Is that a goat?"

"Larry, I'd like to introduce you to Corinne. Corinne, this is Larry. He's single, and he likes goats. Larry, Corinne is single and has a lifetime supply of goats."

"You do?" he asked her. His eyes had a dreamy quality.

The possibility of a woman with a lifetime supply of goats had put him over the edge into happiness. It was like he was seeing the light at the end of the tunnel. An end to his curse.

"You like goats?" she asked him and blushed.

"Do your goats eat clothes?"

"They sure do."

"I don't understand what's going on," Bridget said.

"I'm kind of confused myself," Lucy said.

But Larry and Corinne weren't confused. They walked behind the taco truck and talked, their bodies close to each other. Larry's hammer bulged in his pants pocket, and Corinne's goat chewed gently on Larry's pants leg.

My work was done. Another happy customer. I felt a wave of elation, followed by a definite feeling of power, like I was the Wonder Woman of matchmaking. I could do no wrong.

"Tacos all around!" I announced and slammed a twenty-dollar bill into the hand of the taco truck person.

"Thank you, Gladie. I could go for a few tacos," Bridget said. "Look at my feet. They're twice their normal size. Lech is doing all kinds of things to my body today."

Lucy put her hand around Bridget. "Come on. I'll find us a seat where we can eat our tacos."

"I'll bring them over when they're ready," I said.

As soon as my friends had left, I felt a sharp object in my lower back. "Don't scream. Don't make any sudden movements," I heard. Without turning around, I knew that Arthur Fox was there, and he was whispering threats in my ear. "We're going to move away from the taco truck, and if you don't behave, I'm going to bone you like a duck."

"You can bone a duck?"

He jabbed the knife against my back and I yelped in pain. "Shut up. Not another peep. Come on. We're going to the side street up there."

We walked to the side street. The daffodil show was in high gear with hundreds of people celebrating, but not one of them noticed that Arthur Fox had a knife to my back.

He pushed me into a doorway, and facing me, put the knife at my belly.

"You couldn't help yourself," he said. "You just had to butt in."

"That's the consensus," I said.

"And now it's going to get you killed."

"You're on a run. Four killed. Mike, Joyce, Frank, and now me. That's an impressive number, Johnnie."

"You figured it out, huh?"

"That you're Johnnie Brinkhammer? Yep. I didn't get any of it at first. There were so many suspects. So many jerks. But the underlying truth was that Mike Chantage had done a lot of dirty dealing. He was a dirty cop and a wife stealer. But he also liked to use information for his own profit. Blackmailing. It makes sense that when he recognized you, he didn't alert anyone. Instead, he decided to blackmail you. It was pretty typical of him."

"Bastard thought he could blackmail me," Johnnie said. "I let him believe that he was in charge, that he had power over me. But nobody has power over me."

"So, you stole the liquid daffodil bulbs from your landlord. He probably told you all about daffodils. Morris never shuts up about the flowers. Then, you cooked it in oatmeal cookies, or maybe you just put it in his iced tea earlier in the day. It wouldn't have been hard."

"Mike had a flask. After he dropped dead, I dumped the flask. Nobody ever noticed. Joyce was a simple cup of coffee."

I nodded. "She had figured it all out. You killed a top cop and then had a bunch of other top cops investigating. It was only a matter of time."

Johnnie laughed. "That's not what happened. I thought that Joyce recognized me, but she never did. Since I was the only one who fed her the day she died, she must have figured it out at the end. After that, Frank got a real bee in his bonnet. When I went to his hotel room to offer him my cookies, he caught on. The thing was that there was nothing wrong with the cookies. We got in a fight, and I grabbed the letter opener."

So, Detective Hot Stuff McGruff hadn't killed Frank. Instead, she was just a crappy cop who had touched the murder weapon and then had gone to the bank. It gave me a certain satisfaction to know that she was bad at her job. Spencer wouldn't appreciate a cop being bad at her job, even if she had a perfect body.

"Arthur Fox was one of the two victims of the plane crash, I'm assuming," I said to Johnnie, the man who was calling himself Arthur Fox.

"Can you imagine my luck? The guy wouldn't shut up during the flight. He kept remarking on how much we looked alike and since he had no family, he wondered if maybe we were related."

"And then he dies, and you switched ID's. That was smart, thinking under pressure like that."

His face brightened, and he lowered his hand, which held the knife. "It was a stroke of genius, and it was like God wanted me to live. He wanted me to escape prison. You understand that, right?"

"Sure. Why not?" I said. He wasn't the first killer I had met who thought he was all that.

"You're the last loose end," he said. "Then, I can live happily ever after. Thank you for letting me know where my bitch wife was. That'll be fun to deal with after I finish with you," he said, looking back at the taco truck. Corinne was standing there with the goat. Larry had left and was walking our way. His sleeves were torn off at the shoulders, which I assumed was the work of the goat.

"Hey, Gladie," he called. "I feel great! I can tell the curse is long gone."

Johnnie turned around to face Larry, putting the knife behind his back.

"Are you okay, Gladie?" Larry asked, staring at Johnnie.

"Go get help, Larry! Save yourself!" I yelled, and Johnnie elbowed me in the mouth. A shockwave of pain went through my head, and I stumbled backward, knocking into the door behind me.

"I'll save you, Gladie!" Larry yelled. He took the hammer out of his pocket, and wielding it over his head, ran at Johnnie like he was Jon Snow going after White Walkers.

At that moment, a mob of people dressed in white and each carrying dozens of white daffodils, marched onto our street from the other side, on their way to Main Street, obviously to upset the yellow daffodil show. We were swept up into the group and moved along with them.

Larry was getting further away from us, but Johnnie held on tight to me, the knife always close to me.

"What do we want? White daffodils! When do we want

them? Now!" the group chanted over and over.

We were rushed to the center of Main Street, where Morris and the yellow daffodil supporters met. "How dare you!" I heard Morris yell, and then I saw a white daffodil supporter slap a yellow jumpsuit with a bouquet of flowers.

Then, it was a free for all. It was a slapfest with flowers. Flowers went everywhere. Yellow. White. It was a toss-up who was going to win. Everyone was hitting everyone else with daffodils. With the riot in full swing, Johnnie got control of me again and began to drag me off, presumably to kill me.

"He's got a knife! He's going to kill Gladie!" Larry yelled while getting pulverized by both sides of the daffodil battle.

The word about the knife spread, and like the Red Sea, the daffodil people split, making a large empty circle in the center, with Johnnie and me in the center.

He pulled me tight in front of him and put the knife to my throat. I already had a bloody mouth, which was dripping down my chin.

My hero, Larry, raised the hammer over his head. "I'll save you!" he yelled again, but he was stopped by Spencer, who appeared out of the crowd and grabbed the hammer from Larry's hand. Quiet descended on the street as everyone watched with rapt attention to see what Spencer would do while faced with a killer who had a knife at my throat.

"Here's what's going to happen," Johnnie announced,

loudly, so everyone could hear. "I'm going to take Gladie with me, and once I get out of town, I'll let her go. But if you try anything, I'll slit her throat right here and now."

"Interesting," Spencer said. "What do you think, Peter? You think it's interesting?"

Spencer's brother Peter appeared out of the crowd and stood next to Spencer. "It got my attention, but I enjoy watching the golf channel. So, what do I know?"

"I'm not joking!" Johnnie shouted.

"And yet, you're pretty damned funny," Peter said.

"Not as funny as *Family Guy*, but way above Adam Sandler," Spencer noted.

Bird pushed her way next to Spencer and Peter, and she aimed her gun at Johnnie. "You want me to fill him full of lead?" she asked Spencer.

"Everyone knows your gun is loaded with blanks," Johnnie yelled. "I'm tired of this," he added and held the knife tighter up against my neck, cutting it slightly and making me yelp. Spencer's face grew scarily serious, and in a blur, he launched the hammer through the air.

I watched in horror as the hammer came at my head, and for a moment I thought Spencer was trying to kill me for stealing all of his socks. But it turned out that Spencer was a crack ace hammer thrower. It hit Johnnie square on his forehead, sending him flying backward.

Spencer leapt at me, deflecting the knife with his arm and catching me before I fell along with Johnnie. Peter wasn't far behind. As soon as Johnnie hit the pavement, Peter flipped him over and did a karate move with his arm, completely subduing him.

"Pinky, you're bleeding," Spencer said, cradling my face in his hands.

"So are you," I said, pointing at his hand where he had deflected the knife.

"Did you piss him off, or is he the murderer?"

"Both. He killed your three top cops, and he was pretty pissed off at me for nosing around."

"Can you blame the guy?" Spencer asked. "He has a point."

"You did great, Gladie," Peter said, still immobilizing Johnnie. "I might recruit you for my team."

"Back off, bro," Spencer growled. "Gladie is doing just fine on my team."

"I thought Peter had left to save the world," I said to Spencer.

"He did, and he came back to spend more time with his little brother. Isn't he wonderful?"

"He's pretty good."

"You're going to tell me what happened with my caterer, right?" Spencer asked me.

My stomach growled. "I can tell you all about it, but I'm starving. I gave the taco guy twenty bucks, and he owes me forty tacos."

"I love you, Gladys," Spencer said and kissed my bloody mouth. There was a communal *awwww* sound from the hundreds of people watching the action.

Lucy and Bridget appeared, and Lucy looked madder than spit. "What happened? What happened? Did I miss the action, again? Did you catch the killer while I was sitting with Bridget? Gladie Burger, are you doing this on purpose?"

EPILOGUE

I emptied my basket of sunscreen and antacids onto the counter at the drugstore. I had been packing for a week for my long weekend with Spencer, and I still wasn't finished.

"Can you please hurry up?" the woman behind me complained.

It was Terri Williams, the once powerful detective, who had been demoted to a beat cop. She was standing with her arms crossed and her cart in front of her. There were two tubes of Preparation H in it and a chocolate bar. Oh, how the mighty had fallen.

"Nice to see you, Terri," I said.

"Yeah, right. That'll be the day."

"Can't we try to be friends, or at least be civil to each

other? I did save you from prison, you know."

She narrowed her eyes at me. "What I know is that I was demoted because of you. You and your nosing around. Butting in where you don't belong. Interfering with police business. We'll never be friends. In fact, I'll be watching you, Burger. One step out of line, and I'm going to kick your ass all over this town."

"That hemorrhoid cream would do wonders on those lines by your eyes, you know," I said with a smile and gave the cashier my debit card to pay for the sunscreen. I had hoped that Terri would come around to liking me, but she seemed to hate me more and more each day. A part of me wanted to win her over, but another part of me wanted her hemorrhoids to swell. I was still concerned about her crush on Spencer, but for now, I didn't see her as big of a threat as she was before. Perhaps it was because I was going to go on vacation with Spencer, and I had just had my entire body waxed.

I left the drugstore and walked over to Tea Time to get a latte. As I opened the door, a Rolls Royce drove up and stopped at the curb. The window opened, and Corinne stuck her head out. She had had her hair dyed, and she looked twenty years younger. She was also smiling ear to ear, happy as a clam.

"Hey, Gladie," she said. "Larry wants to talk to you."

I closed the door to Tea Time and walked up to the car. Crouching down by the passenger door, I looked inside. Larry was dressed to the nines. All of his hair had grown back, and he looked right as rain. "Sweet ride, Larry," I said. "When did you get this?"

"My ship has come in, Gladie. I had invested in a pig farm, and it went public. I'm rich!"

"That's wonderful," I said.

"Corinne and I are off to Reno to get married, and we just wanted to thank you one more time."

He hadn't stopped thanking me since I matched him with Corinne. He had already paid me for my services and given me a gift of a fancy Italian espresso machine.

"Congratulations, both of you. I hope you have a wonderful time in Reno."

"We will. Those goats have kept me healthy, wealthy, and wise," Larry said. "I've lost ten pounds, my cholesterol is normal for the first time in years, and my willy acts like it's eighteen years old."

We said goodbye, and I watched them drive away to their nuptials in Reno. It had turned out that Cynthia and Sidney had also gotten married in Reno and left on a long cruise. They had sent me word after Johnnie, aka Arthur, had been caught, and they apologized for leaving so abruptly but explained to me how afraid they had been for their lives.

Spencer had been in a wonderful mood in the past week. With Remington back in town, he was free to go on vacation with me, and he was still glowing from having his brother around for a few days. Peter had left to save the world, again, but he promised to visit, soon.

I guessed the world needed a lot of saving.

Carrying my latte in a to-go cup, I walked home. Official-looking "Do not cross" tape was wrapped around the house across the street because the house was now condemned. The airplane had been sent away somewhere, and the catastrophe tourists were long gone.

I was surprised to see Spencer across the street, facing the condemned house. I joined him, slipping my hand around his waist and leaning in against him.

"I think this house has a lot of potential," he said.

I froze. Was he going to ask me the big question? What would I say?

"What do you think about the house?" he asked me.

"I think it might be cursed."

"Really? I guess we could get a couple goats to gnaw at the baseboards. That should clear it up, right?" Goats might have worked for Larry, but I wasn't so sure they would work for a house. But he was talking about "we." What did that mean exactly?

"We could get a couple goats? What are you saying, Spencer?"

He gave me a squeeze. "We'll talk about it on our

vacation."

The End

Don't miss **It Happened One Fright**, *the next book in the Matchmaker Mysteries.*

And don't forget to sign up for the newsletter for new releases and special deals: http://www.elisesax.com/mailing-list.php

ABOUT THE AUTHOR

Elise Sax worked as a journalist for fifteen years, mostly in Paris, France. She took a detour from journalism and became a private investigator before writing her first novel. She lives in Southern California with her two sons.

She loves to hear from her readers. Don't hesitate to contact her at elisesax@gmail.com, and sign up for her newsletter at http://elisesax.com/mailing-list.php to get notifications of new releases and sales.

Elisesax.com
https://www.facebook.com/ei.sax.9
@theelisesax

CPSIA information can be obtained
at www.ICGtesting.com
Printed in the USA
LVHW110312070722
722935LV00018B/368